MISCHIEF AT CAMP

The Saddle Club was having a meeting after dinner. "I can't believe these girls," Carole began. "They are so convinced they're going to win all the ribbons at the show next week just because they won them before. And that they deserve them! Ugh, I *hate* that kind of snobbishness."

"So do I," Lisa said. "So does almost everybody. But what can we do? I mean it's not as if we can change them."

"Why not?" Carole asked. "I mean why not try to change them? These girls think they're going to win all the ribbons, right?"

Lisa and Stevie nodded.

"So, we don't let them. *We* win them all instead. That'll show them!"

Her friends grinned wickedly. Carole continued, "What we've got to do is to *look* like we're bumbling beginners. You know, we'll make dumb mistakes so they can feel superior. Then, when the time comes— whammo! We'll take all the blues!"

"What a fabulous idea!" Lisa laughed. "I think I feel a Saddle Club project coming on!"

THE SADDLE CLUB

RIDING CAMP

BONNIE BRYANT

A BANTAM SKYLARK BOOK®
NEW YORK · TORONTO · LONDON · SYDNEY · AUCKLAND

I would like to express my special thanks to Don De-
Marzio for his help to me.

—B.B.

RL S, 009–012

RIDING CAMP
A Bantam Skylark Book / April 1990

Skylark Books is a registered trademark of Bantam Books,
a division of Bantam Doubleday Dell Publishing Group, Inc.
Registered in U.S. Patent and Trademark Office and elsewhere.

"The Saddle Club" is a trademark of Bonnie
Bryant Hiller. The Saddle Club design/logo, which
consists of an inverted U-shaped design, a riding crop,
and a riding hat, is a trademark of Bantam Books.

ISBN 0-553-15790-6

Published simultaneously in the United States and Canada

Bantam Books are published by Bantam Books, a division of Bantam
Doubleday Dell Publishing Group, Inc. Its trademark, consisting of the
words "Bantam Books" and the portrayal of a rooster, is Registered in U.S.
Patent and Trademark Office and in other countries. Marca Registrada. Bantam Books, 666 Fifth Avenue, New York, New York 10103.

PRINTED IN THE UNITED STATES OF AMERICA

CWO   0 9 8 7 6 5 4 3 2 1

For Penelope B. Carey

1

"WATCH HOW SHE does this," Carole Hanson said to
Lisa Atwood. The two girls were standing in the pas-
sageway outside a stall at Pine Hollow Stables. Stevie
Lake was inside the stall preparing Topside for a trip.

Carole, Lisa, and Stevie were best friends. They'd
gotten to know each other at Pine Hollow and had
formed a group called The Saddle Club. The club had
only two rules, and they were easy ones: All the members had to be horse crazy, and they had to be willing
to help one another. So far the three girls were the
only active members of the club, although there were a
few out-of-state friends who were honorary members.

Stevie finished fastening the final protective leg
wrap on the big bay gelding horse, patted Topside reas-

suringly, and stood up. She clipped a lead rope onto Topside's halter and looked him square in the eye.

"Pine Hollow's Flight One to Moose Hill Riding Camp is now ready for boarding," she announced. "All passengers holding first-class tickets may proceed to the gate. And that means you."

Outside the stable, a horse van was waiting to take Topside to Moose Hill, the riding camp Stevie would be attending for the next two weeks. Stevie had been lucky. A friend of hers had won the camp session in a raffle, but since she didn't like riding very much, she'd offered it to Stevie. Horse-crazy Stevie didn't understand her friend at all, but under the circumstances, she decided it was just fine that her friend didn't like riding.

"I'm almost too excited to watch," Lisa told Carole. "I can't believe it. Two solid weeks of horses, horses, and horses. Nothing but horses!"

Carole nodded, her eyes wide with excitement.

"I can't believe how lucky we all are!" Stevie said.

"I still don't understand how you managed to convince Max to pay our way. How did you get him to sponsor us?"

There was a sparkle in Stevie's eye. Convincing people, especially Max Regnery, the owner of Pine Hollow Stables, to do things they might not actually *want* to do was one of her specialties. "It was easy," she said airily, dismissing Carole's admiration. "A mere sleight of hand."

"More like sleight of mouth, if I know you," Carole added.

"Yeah, more like that," Stevie agreed, returning to her normal self. "Now let's see if I can do a sleight of hoof and get Topside onto the van."

She turned her attention to the horse. Topside was an experienced traveler. He was a championship show horse and had performed all over the world. Max had recently bought him when the horse's owner, Dorothy DeSoto, had been forced to give up competitive riding because of an accident. Now Topside was going to riding camp with The Saddle Club to get a new kind of show experience. The two-week session at Moose Hill would end with a horse show for the campers. It would be completely different from what Topside had known before, and Max had felt it would be good for both Stevie and Topside to try it together.

Carole and Lisa would be riding horses assigned to them from the camp's own stable. They loved the horses they usually rode at Pine Hollow, but Max couldn't spare two more horses for the session. Both girls also knew that it would be a good opportunity for them to try training on different horses.

"Come on, boy," Stevie said. She clucked her tongue and led Topside toward the stall door. Carole slid the door back to let them out. Stevie held the lead rope with one hand and a pail containing Topside's grooming gear with the other. She looked over her shoulder at the horse. He seemed to sense that something was up and twitched his tail excitedly. Stevie grinned over her shoulder at him, still leading him straight out of the stall.

"Stevie, watch your head!" Carole warned. It was too late, though. With a thunk, Stevie's head connected with the fire extinguisher on the wall of the stable opposite Topside's stall.

Stevie made a face and rubbed her head where she'd hit it. Then she crossed her eyes. Lisa giggled. Stevie had the ability to make almost anything funny. It was one of the things Lisa liked the best—and that sometimes annoyed her the most—about Stevie.

"Are you okay?" Lisa asked.

"Never mind her—what about the fire extinguisher?" Carole said, adjusting the big red metal canister. Stevie glared at Carole briefly.

Lisa laughed. She knew Carole was concerned about Stevie's bump, but it was just like her to be equally concerned with the safety of the horses. Just as Stevie could always see the funny side of a situation, Carole could always see the serious side—when it came to horses. It was Lisa's feeling that Stevie and Carole balanced each other. Sometimes that was a problem, since it meant Lisa was right smack in the middle. But most of the time it was a lot of fun.

"Come on, you guys," Lisa said. "The sooner we get Topside on the van the sooner we can leave for camp."

Carole began clucking at Topside, encouraging him to follow Stevie toward the van.

"I guess that means my job is to bring the tack, huh?" Lisa asked.

"Thanks." Stevie grinned.

Lisa walked toward the stable's tack room. It was one of her favorite places in Pine Hollow. At first glance, it was a mess. The room was covered with snaking leather straps hanging every which way and an endless row of saddles that required constant soaping and cleaning. That was the way it had first looked to Lisa when she'd started riding at Pine Hollow. After a few days, however, she'd learned that there was a strict order to everything. Each saddle was in a place that corresponded to its horse's stall. A matching bridle hung above each saddle. Spare leathers, carefully sorted by size, hung along another wall. There were buckets for metal parts, bits, chains, buckles, hooks, and rings, which were all meticulously grouped.

In fact, the whole room was organized very carefully. It just didn't look that way. Lisa wondered, as she looked at it now, how she could ever have thought it was messy. She quickly located Topside's tack and picked it up to carry it to the van.

It was exciting, and a little frightening, to think that she was about to become familiar with a new stable, a new horse, and new riders. Lisa, unlike Carole and Stevie, had begun riding just a few months ago. She didn't have as much experience as her friends did. She was sure she would enjoy Moose Hill, but she still felt a little uneasy. There was only one thing to do about that. Lisa hefted the saddle, adjusting its weight, and left the tack room.

There was nobody inside the stable. Everyone was watching Stevie load Topside. There was one last thing Lisa wanted to do before she left. Pine Hollow Stables had been around for a long time and had developed a lot of traditions. One of those was its good-luck horseshoe. By tradition, every rider at Pine Hollow touched it before going for a ride. Nobody was sure when the tradition had begun, or why, but everybody knew that no rider at Pine Hollow had ever been seriously hurt in a riding accident. Lisa glanced around. She felt a little silly, but she still wanted to do it. The horseshoe was nailed up by the door to the indoor ring. When she reached the doorway to the ring, she set Topside's tack on the ledge of an empty stall, stood on tiptoe, and reached up high, brushing the horseshoe with her fingers. The feeling of the smooth, worn iron comforted her.

She picked up the tack again and carried it through the stable to where the van and the station wagon and her friends were waiting for her.

Stevie had loaded Topside into the trailer by the time Lisa joined her friends and the crowd gathered in the driveway. Red O'Malley, Pine Hollow's most trusted stablehand, was driving Topside to Moose Hill. It seemed to Lisa that she and her friends were just being allowed to hitch a ride with the horse!

"Have we got all our stuff in the back of the car?" Carole asked, peering through the station wagon's dusty windows.

"I think we've got it all," Red said dryly. "Including the kitchen sink."

Carole was famous for forgetting important things, like clothes, when she went on trips, but the gigantic pile of luggage in the car indicated that she hadn't forgotten anything this time, since everything in the world was probably already crammed in the bags.

Finally it was time to go. The girls climbed into the station wagon and rolled down their windows so they could wave to their parents, their fellow students, Max, and his mother, Mrs. Reg. Before they were out of the driveway, Max was shooing the other riders back inside. It was almost time for class to begin, and as far as Max was concerned, there were no good excuses for class to begin late.

"I don't think anything would keep Max from starting class on time," Lisa remarked.

"Oh, maybe a tornado," Stevie said.

"Not unless it leveled the barn," Carole added.

Lisa giggled. She was glad that Max was so serious about riding instruction. She hoped her teacher at camp would be as good.

"I'm a little nervous," she confessed to her friends. "I mean, you guys have been riding for years. You're used to other horses and other instructors. Pine Hollow is practically the only place I've ever ridden. Is it going to be okay?"

"You bet it is," Carole assured her. "Not only is it going to be okay, it's going to be great. It's important to have different experiences. And besides, you *have* ridden other places. Remember the Devines' dude ranch? And New York? Now those were *really* different. Moose Hill's going to be much more like Pine Hollow than those were."

"Not exactly," Stevie said. "Did you read the brochure carefully? I mean, did you read the part about one stablehand for every five riders? That's not quite like Pine Hollow, where there are only two stablehands for the whole stable and all the work is done by the poor overworked riders, who have to muck out the stalls and clean the tack and groom the horses while the stablehands hardly ever lift a finger. Right, Red?"

Red snorted in response. It was true that the riders did a lot of work around Pine Hollow. It was one way the stable kept expenses down and made riding something more people could do. However, horses were a lot of work, and no matter how much the riders pitched in, there was plenty for Red and his co-workers to do. The girls knew that as well as he did.

"Go on," Red said. "Have yourselves a real vacation at this camp, but don't come back to us too good to groom your own horses, okay? One of those is enough at the stable, thank you very much."

Red didn't have to name names. He was talking about Veronica diAngelo, the stable's spoiled little rich girl.

"Don't worry, Red," Lisa assured him. "Nothing, short of about ten million dollars, would make us as obnoxious as she is."

"Twenty," he said, and then turned all his attention to his driving. Lisa wasn't certain if Red had meant it would take twenty million dollars to make *her* obnoxious or if he thought twenty million was what Veronica had. She watched the hilly Virginia countryside slide by and thought about what she'd do with twenty million dollars. She'd build a stable for herself and buy a horse. Two horses. No, one for every member of The Saddle Club. She'd hire loads of stablehands and she'd ride with her friends all day, every day. They'd enter all kinds of competitions and they'd win them all, because when the three of them were teamed together, they couldn't lose. She'd have a swimming pool—two actually: one indoor, one outdoor. She'd have a thick pile carpet in her room and her very own maid to pick up any of the expensive clothes she happened to drop on the floor. But, she told herself, she'd still take care of her own horse, and she'd never be as obnoxious as Veronica.

"Did you see her face?!" Stevie shrieked, abruptly bringing Lisa out of her daydream. Carole was laughing.

Lisa had no idea what they were talking about. "Who?" she asked.

"Veronica," Carole said. "You know, when she sat on the moldy hay. Didn't you see that?"

"Oh, yeah, I did. She kept swiping at the seat of her *designer* breeches. It was very funny and the harder she swiped, the angrier Max got." Lisa smiled, remembering the scene.

"Well, Max had left the hay bale out so that the salesman could see what he'd delivered, and Veronica just assumed it was a new throne for the princess."

"Got what she deserved," Lisa said. "A moldy

throne. Well, better her breeches than a horse's manger!"

"Absolutely!" Carole said seriously. "Horses have very delicate stomachs and moldy hay can cause colic, and that's no joke. To a horse, colic can be fatal! So if all that happened with that bale was that Veronica's pants had to go to the dry cleaner, well, we were just plain lucky."

"It's not so much luck as it is caution, you know," Red said. "Moldy hay will happen. You just have to test for it with every shipment and every bale."

"How do you do that?" Lisa asked.

"You feel it and see if there's any moisture, then you sniff at it for a funny odor."

"You can feel it for warmth, too," Carole said.

"Well, if it's warm, you're in real trouble," Red said. "That means that there's so much decay going on inside that it's heating up to burn. You want to get it far away from the barn as soon as possible. Those things can just about explode."

"You know one of the things I love about horses?" Lisa asked, thinking out loud. "I love the fact that there's so much to find out about them that you can learn about them no matter where you are or what you're doing, like in a car driving over the hills of Virginia. You can learn just as much out of the saddle as you can in it."

"It's just that it's more fun if you're in it," Stevie said, and the girls agreed.

"I have the feeling we'll be there any minute now," Carole said.

"Yep," Red agreed, turning the car and its trailer off the main road where the sign pointed to Moose Hill.

The road was narrow and shaded by tall maples, which made it suddenly cool in the hot August afternoon. Gradually the surrounding forest became pine and the road turned into a dirt trail. Red slowed down so the van wouldn't bounce in the ruts. After a half-mile, they saw a horse gate. Stevie jumped out of the car to open and close it for them. She clasped the latch carefully behind the trailer and rejoined her friends. Red drove them up a long hill on the winding road and then, as if it grew from the forest, there stood before them the stately red barn of Moose Hill Riding Camp.

2

"I THINK HE said our cabin was this one—the second one on the right." Lisa pointed to a small wooden bunkhouse. "Yeah, here it is, Number Three." She paused to readjust the weight of the three heavy bags she was carrying. Carole did the same.

"I hope Stevie knows what a wonderful thing we're doing for her, lugging her stuff while she checks Topside into his suite at the Hilton on the Hill." Lisa and Carole had agreed to carry Stevie's things for her while she got Topside settled in. They were both beginning to think Stevie had gotten the best of the deal. When they heard Stevie shout gaily from behind them, they were sure of it.

"Here I come!" Stevie announced her arrival. "And, hey, thanks for all the help. Boy, you won't believe the barn! It's really wild. It's a big old farmer's barn with a few stalls—most of the time the horses are in the paddock—and this gigantic hayloft. It'll be a blast to mess around in."

"If we can move at all after carrying all this weight," Carole said pointedly.

Stevie got the hint. She took her bags from Carole and Lisa and followed them into the cabin.

The screen door slammed behind them. The girls found themselves standing inside a very plain rectangular room with a bathroom off to the side. There were six cots in the room, each with a cubby area with shelves for clothes and personal belongings. Lisa looked dubiously at her two large duffel bags while her eyes adjusted to the dim light cast by the single overhead bulb. She was sure she'd never fit all her belongings into the modest cubby.

"That one's my bed," an unfamiliar voice said to her. There was nothing friendly or warm about the greeting.

"Oh," Lisa said, startled. She turned to see a girl about her own age emerging from the bathroom. "I wasn't going to take your bed. I was just looking at how small the cubbies are. I was thinking about . . . ." She was going to explain about how her mother always packed too much for her when she realized that the girl who had spoken wasn't listening. She'd picked up her riding hat and was striding out of the cabin.

"Hello to you, too!" Stevie said. The only response she got was the clatter of the girl's boots going down the steps of the cabin.

"Whew!" Carole remarked.

"Don't mind Debbie," another voice spoke. A girl they hadn't noticed before was sitting in a corner of the room, saddle-soaping her boots. "She just found out that Elsa, who won just about all the blue ribbons in the show last year, not only came back this year, but is in this cabin. My name's Nora."

For a second, The Saddle Club girls were too stunned to speak, or to return the introduction. It would never have occurred to any of them to be upset about bunking with a blue-ribbon winner. In fact, Carole was really excited about the idea of being able to spend extra time with somebody who knew more than she did and could teach her.

Then the girls composed themselves and made introductions. Nora showed them which beds were theirs and even helped Lisa figure out how to stuff all her things into the small cubby.

"Where's the blue-ribbon winner?" Carole asked Nora as the two of them put the sheets and blankets on her cot. Elsa's cot was next to Carole's and her duffel bags were there, but none of her gear was stowed and her bed wasn't made.

"Well, if I know Elsa," Nora began, "she's found a

private area in the field, out of sight of the barn and the main house, and she's working with her horse."

"You mean campers are allowed to ride without any supervision and no riding partner?" Carole asked, surprised. There was no way Max would let a young rider out alone. Even the best of them had to have a friend along, just in case.

"Campers aren't supposed to do that, but Elsa does it anyway," Nora answered.

"But it's so much more fun to be with friends," Stevie said.

"There are two things wrong with that," Nora said. "In the first place, nobody is Elsa's friend, and secondly, she wouldn't want to ride with somebody who might learn something from her. She's made it crystal clear that she intends to take home all the blue ribbons again this year."

"Oh, yuck." Stevie made a face.

"You know, that reminds me of what Kate Devine said about all the really good riders she used to compete with," Carole said. Kate was a junior championship rider who had quit competition because of people like Debbie and Elsa.

"You know Kate Devine?" Nora asked, her jaw dropping.

"Sure, she's an old friend of ours," Carole said. "Her dad and mine are Marine Corps buddies. In fact, just a while back, the three of us visited her on her parents' dude ranch. She's learned to ride Western and she loves it." Carole tucked in the final sheet, smoothed the blanket with her hand, and dropped a quarter on the bed to see if it would bounce the way it was supposed to in the Marine Corps. It didn't. She didn't care. She pocketed the quarter. "Let's go see the rest of the camp," she said to her friends.

"Want the grand tour?" Nora asked. "Listen, lunch starts in a half an hour. I can show you everything by then if you want."

That sounded pretty good to Carole. She'd only gotten a glimpse of the camp on the way in. "That'd be great," Carole said, speaking for Stevie and Lisa too. "We're almost done here—"

"I have an errand up at the barn," Nora said quickly. "Meet me up there, okay? You know where that is?"

"Yeah, the big red building with all the hay and the horses?" Stevie asked innocently.

"Don't mind her," Lisa said to Nora. "She jokes about everything. We'll see you up at the barn in five minutes."

Nora nodded and left The Saddle Club alone in the cabin.

"What a place," Stevie remarked, stuffing her belongings into the tiny cubby by her cot. "It's got all the ingredients to be the most wonderful place in the world—horses and kids who love horses—and we end up in a cabin with a riding whiz who keeps the secret of her success and a would-be whiz who won't talk to anybody!" She crammed her toothbrush in the last available space and stood up, looking at her friends for sympathy.

"I think the way to handle people like Debbie and Elsa is to ignore them. And since they seem willing to ignore us, it won't be hard to do," Lisa said.

"Yeah, and Nora seems nice enough," Carole reminded Stevie.

"Just watch out that she doesn't try to learn *our* riding secrets!" Stevie joked.

"As far as I'm concerned, she can have all my riding secrets," Carole said. "The only real secret to riding is that it's fun. I have a feeling that there are a few people around here who haven't learned that yet."

There were many ways in which the three members of The Saddle Club were very different, but that was one thing they agreed on completely. Lisa smiled to herself, thinking about all the fun riding she had ahead of her.

"I hate to change the subject from horses, guys," Carole continued, "but did the two of you happen to notice what I noticed down the hill?"

"More cabins?" Lisa asked. She'd seen a second cluster of cabins like the one they were in.

"Not just *more* cabins," Carole said. "*Boys'* cabins. The camp's coed, remember?"

"Yeah, right, big deal," Stevie said, sitting on her freshly made bed. "Pine Hollow's coed, too. The trouble is that if nine out of ten guys are cute, the tenth one rides at Pine Hollow. I have absolutely no interest in any boy who rides horses. I've never met one who wasn't a complete creep."

Lisa was a little surprised by the conviction in Stevie's voice. It was true that the guys who rode at Pine Hollow weren't exactly cute, but there was always a chance you'd find the right one, wasn't there? "Oh, come on, Stevie," she said. "Maybe Moose Hill is different."

"Fat chance," Stevie said. "You should have seen the guy who came in when I was putting Topside in the barn. He ordered everybody around like he was a male version of Veronica diAngelo!"

"So, maybe he's rich?" Lisa suggested. "I could learn to love a rich man."

Stevie gave her a withering look. "Not this one," she said. "Unless you really go for short, fat, and ugly as well. In that case, we've found Mr. Right for you."

"Well, what about the tall guy who held Topside's saddle for you?" Carole asked.

"That drip?" Stevie scoffed. "Oh, I admit that when I first saw him I thought he was kind of cute, but I asked him what his name was and he couldn't seem to remember. I'm telling you, the boys here are no better than the girls. Stick to the horses!" She grinned and stood up. All three girls had finished with their unpacking and were ready to meet Nora at the barn.

"Did you at least have a chance to meet some of the horses?" Lisa asked. "After all, I guess that's what we're here for."

"The horses are something else," Stevie said, leading the way out of the cabin. "There's a chestnut gelding who's a real beauty. He's got this incredible arch to his neck—I think there's some Arabian there—and he holds his tail high, like he's so proud of himself. He came over to me first thing and sort of hugged me. But then this paint mare got jealous and started prancing around the paddock so I'd notice her. Meanwhile two bays were pawing at the ground, like they'd seen the mare's act before and they were bored with it. And all this time Topside is watching, taking it all in."

All the way to the top of the hill, Stevie continued telling her friends about the horses. Lisa was so excited to be at Moose Hill she could barely contain herself. She decided Stevie was right. The girls didn't seem very nice and the boys were probably losers. It was a good thing the horses were so terrific!

3

WHEN NORA GAVE the girls their grand tour of the grounds, they found that the camp was basically laid out in an oval. The massive barn stood at one end of the grounds. The barn had paddocks on two sides, one at the upper level, one below. The lower one was connected to a stable area. There was a drive-in entrance on the third side of the barn, and an outdoor riding ring on the fourth. Beyond the riding ring was a huge grassy area about the size of a football field, where the riders could play mounted games like shadow tag. The mess hall stood on one side of the field; the rec hall was directly across from it. A regular sports field next to the rec hall provided space for unmounted games like softball or Frisbee.

The cabins were down the hill from the barn. The

boys' and girls' cabins lay on opposite shores of the swimming pond, separated from it by a small sandy beach. A short dirt road led from the barn to the cabin area. Other foot trails led through the woods directly to the pond and the mess hall.

The main area of the camp was an open space, with just a few trees around the edges of the paddocks and riding arenas. There was a shaded area behind the mess hall with picnic tables, where most meals were served in good weather. The cabins were in the woods, cooled by tall trees.

"The camp has about thirty riders at a time," Nora explained. "Usually, there are about twenty girls and ten boys. I think that's how many Barry said there were now."

Barry, they had learned, was the camp director. The girls had met him up at the stable, where he'd been overseeing the arrival of several horses. He'd been so busy telling the stablehands what to do that he'd barely acknowledged their presence. Carole had been very surprised that one of the stablehands needed so much supervision. His name was Fred and he didn't seem to know much at all. Carole made a mental note not to let Fred near her horse.

"Well, that's about it," Nora said to The Saddle Club girls. "Unless you want to tour the grain-storage area on the other side of the upper paddock, we're done."

"Thanks a lot for showing us around," Lisa said. "It seemed so confusing at first, but I think I can find my way around now."

"Oh, no problem," Nora told them. "It was fun. Listen, I'm supposed to help set the tables today, so I'm going over to the mess hall. You should come too, when the bell rings, okay? I'll see you there."

The girls agreed to meet Nora at the mess hall. Lisa and Carole wanted to wash up before lunch, but Stevie thought she ought to check on Topside one more time. They decided to regroup at lunchtime.

Stevie wasn't sure if the pond or the barn was her favorite part of the camp. There was something really wonderful about the barn. The thing about it was that it *was* a barn, not really a stable. The horses spent most of their time turned out into the paddocks or the field beyond them. The stabling area in the lower level was more like a resting place for sick or injured horses. It had a separate entrance for the horses from the lower paddock. The farrier—the blacksmith who put shoes on the horses—worked there as well, and horses in need of shoes were kept overnight in the stable area.

The upper level of the building, like most barns, had a sort of drive-through, convenient for delivery and pickup of feed and equipment. Large storage rooms stood on both sides of the drive-through.

Once Stevie had assured herself that Topside was doing just fine, she checked out the storage rooms. One, of course, was a tack room. Like Pine Hollow's tack room, at first glance it looked like a disaster area. But Stevie was pretty sure that there was an underlying order there, just the same as there was at Pine Hollow.

She looked to see where Topside's tack had been stowed by the stablehand. She didn't see it at first, but when she did finally find it, she wasn't so sure about the room's underlying order. Topside's tack had been dumped in a corner of the room—on the floor! Stevie was furious. She picked up the saddle and put it on the nearest saddle rack. Then she untangled Topside's bridle and laid it across the seat of the saddle, since the tack hook above the saddle rack was broken. She moved aside the stack of leathers that had been carelessly cast on the floor beneath the saddle rack and neatly stacked Topside's personal grooming gear there.

When she finished, Stevie grimly studied the rest of the tack room with a new skepticism. She now had the feeling that, unlike Pine Hollow's tack room, this one not only looked like a mess, but *was* a mess. So much for the highly touted stablehands of Moose Hill. And so much for her vacation from grooming! She'd take care of her own horse and gear, and she'd tell her friends to do the same.

When Stevie emerged from the tack room, she realized that there were no campers or staff members around. That could only mean one thing—and the grumbling in her stomach confirmed it. The lunch bell must have rung and she hadn't heard it. She found a cold-water spigot at the back of the barn and quickly washed her hands, wiping them dry on her jeans.

"Mess hall, mess hall," Stevie said to herself. "It's one of the buildings on either side of the riding field. But which one?" She guessed left. She was wrong. It took her almost ten minutes to figure out where the mess hall was. She felt totally stupid walking up to the picnic tables. Here she was, ready to start eating, and all the campers were working on their desserts.

She felt even more stupid when she realized that there wasn't a seat for her at the table where Carole, Lisa, and Nora were eating.

"I'm sorry. We tried to save you a seat, but someone took it," Carole said pointedly. She nodded toward Elsa, who was sitting next to Lisa and eating in sullen silence.

"It happens." Stevie shrugged. She almost felt sorry for her friends. She knew she wouldn't like eating with such a sourpuss. She looked around for another seat.

There was only one left, and just looking at it made Stevie's face redden. The sole remaining seat in the entire picnic area was at a table that was filled with boys. If she hadn't been starving, she might have skipped lunch altogether. But, she reminded herself, she'd spent her life eating with boys—even if they were only her brothers. Resigned, she walked over to the table.

"This seat taken?" she asked.

Seven boys looked up at her, apparently too surprised to answer. It annoyed Stevie to have to ask twice. "*¿Esta el seato es libro?*" she asked in totally fractured Spanish, responding to their rudeness with her own.

Six boys stared at her as if she'd just sprouted another head. The seventh burst into laughter.

"*Muy libro,*" he answered in equally bad Spanish. "Sit down." Stevie did.

It turned out that she was sitting across the table from the boy who had answered her question. She was inclined to like people who laughed when she was funny, so she took a minute to look at this one. Then it was her turn to be surprised. This guy, who had already proved that he was smart by laughing at her joke, was also unmistakably cute. He had short, light brown hair and intense green eyes. He was tall, with broad shoulders and a deep summer tan. What she noticed most, though, was his smile. It was welcoming and friendly. And best of all, it was directed at her.

"Hi, I'm Phil Marston," he said. He smiled again.

"I'm Stevie Lake," she said, stumbling over her own name. What was the matter with her?

"You from around here?" Phil asked, and the conversation began. It turned out that he came from a town about ten miles from Willow Creek, where Stevie lived. She had heard of the stable where he rode. He was a year older than she was. He hadn't been riding quite as long, but he had more show experience. It turned out that they had a lot in common. They both liked riding and jumping. They were both interested in dressage. They both hated math. Phil thought he had too many sisters. Stevie said she had too many brothers. They had each brought a horse to camp. But while Stevie's belonged to Pine Hollow, Phil had his own horse, a bay gelding named Teddy, after Theodore Roosevelt because, Phil explained, when he had first gotten him, the horse was a rough rider.

Stevie laughed at Phil's jokes. Phil laughed at Stevie's. Neither noticed when the other boys at the table finished their lunch and left. They didn't even notice when Carole and Lisa arrived, until Carole announced their presence by clearing her throat several times.

"Ahem!" Carole grunted, sitting down next to Stevie. Lisa sat next to Carole.

"Oh, hi!" Stevie welcomed her friends. She introduced them to Phil. He smiled and nodded at them, but, Stevie noticed, he smiled even more at her. She liked that. She smiled back.

"I think we have a class to go to," Carole said.

"We do?" Stevie said. It seemed impossible that lunch could be over so fast. After all, she'd just sat down at the table a few minutes ago, hadn't she? She looked at her watch. It had been almost forty-five minutes.

"Do you have the same class we do now?" Stevie asked Phil, not even knowing what her class was.

It turned out that Phil had a jump class. The girls were having a flat class, so they might not see each other again for a long time—at least not until dinner, which was five hours away.

"Come on!" Carole commanded, tugging at Stevie's sleeve. "We have to change into our riding clothes, go to the stable, tack up our horses, and who knows what all else, all in about fifteen minutes."

"Carole's right," Lisa said. "And Phil has to do the same thing for his class, too. We've all got to get rolling."

"Okay," Phil agreed. He stood up. "I hope there'll be a *seato libro* next to you at supper tonight," he told Stevie. "And, uh, you too," he added politely to

Carole and Lisa. Then he waved and jogged off toward his cabin.

Stevie had the strangest sensation. It was funny, but it was also very nice. Her stomach was fluttering and her knees felt soft. "I feel weak," she said.

Carole and Lisa exchanged glances.

"Is this from the same girl who lectured us a couple hours ago about how all the boys who ride horses are drips and creeps?" Lisa teased.

"I think it's time to concentrate on horses," Carole said sensibly. "After all, that's what we're here for, isn't it?"

"Speak for yourself," Stevie said, sighing contentedly. It took Carole a second to realize that Stevie was joking.

Lisa looked at her watch. "Twelve minutes," she announced, and they still had to change their clothes. They didn't jog casually to their cabin the way Phil had—they ran!

LISA WAS VERY excited and more than a little nervous to be in her first riding class at riding camp. She had never had a lesson from anybody other than Max Regnery and she didn't know what to expect. She was glad her two best friends were with her. She mounted her camp horse, a bay gelding named Major, and took him out into the ring.

Barry had all the riders form a large circle in the ring. Then he invited them to introduce themselves and their horses and tell about their riding experience. Lisa could hardly believe the stories the other students told. Ribbons here, cups there, championships everywhere—were *any* of these people beginners? She swallowed nervously.

"And you?" Barry said, pointing to her.

Lisa had taken a public speaking course in school and had gotten an A in it. But she'd never had a public-speaking assignment that included confessing to a circle of people, most of them strangers, that she didn't have much experience as a rider. She didn't know how to begin. She cleared her throat, stalling for time.

"Um, my name's Lisa Atwood. I'm riding a horse named, uh, Major. I come from Willow Creek, Virginia, and I just started riding a few months ago." She stared down at the ground.

"Any prizes or ribbons you'd like to tell us about?" Barry asked.

"Prizes?" Lisa repeated as if she'd never heard the word. Barry nodded encouragement. "Well, I guess, maybe. Um, my team won a gymkhana. Does that count?"

A few riders tittered. Lisa wanted to die.

"I think you're holding back on us, Lisa," Barry said. "I spoke to Max Regnery about you. He says you are a very promising student. He expects great things of you. You may not have any ribbons yet, but it won't be long." Lisa turned bright red.

Some students continued to stare at her, but now Lisa felt better about it. Maybe she didn't have as much experience as most of the others, but she had potential. She just wished she could hang it in a cabinet on the wall.

Carole introduced herself and her horse, Basil. She'd been riding long enough that the other students respected her without support from Barry.

Then it was Stevie's turn. One look at Stevie and Lisa knew she would be in trouble. Stevie obviously hadn't heard a word anybody had said. She had a dreamy, faraway look in her eyes that could mean only one thing: Love.

"Hey, you!" Barry said, waving his arms to catch Stevie's attention. It didn't work. Carole reached her hand over to pinch her. Stevie absently brushed Carole's hand away.

"Stevie!" Carole hissed. "It's your turn! Time to introduce yourself and Topside."

Suddenly, Stevie looked panicked. She'd missed everything that was going on and had no idea what to say.

"Cough," Carole whispered, reaching over as if to help her friend. "Cough hard."

Obediently, Stevie began hacking. She was so convincing, she looked as if she were choking.

Carole thumped her gently on the back, trying to look as if she were helping her friend through a difficult coughing fit. "This is my friend Stevie Lake," she said. "Like Lisa and me, Stevie rides at Pine Hollow. She's been riding since she was eight. She's been in a lot of local shows and has a cabinet full of ribbons. There's one trophy there, but I think it's pretty dusty, so it might have been Best Beginner when she was eight and she doesn't take it very seriously. She's riding Topside, who used to belong to Dorothy DeSoto. Pine Hollow bought him from her when she retired from competitive riding. Are you okay now, Stevie?" Carole asked sweetly, now that Stevie's "fit" had stopped.

"I'm just fine, thank you, Carole. Just fine."

"Fully recovered?" Carole asked significantly.

"Mmm-hmm," Stevie said. "Thanks for the help."

Whatever else was going on in Stevie's mind, and Lisa suspected that a lot was going on in there, Lisa knew two things for sure: Stevie had learned her lesson about daydreaming in class, and Carole was a true friend—and a fast thinker!

4

AFTER CLASS, LISA dismounted and led Major to the barn, where he could be cross-tied and untacked. Some horses were likely to move when you were trying to work on them, so it always made sense to hook a rope on either side of the horse's halter to keep the movement to a minimum. So far, Lisa and Major were getting along pretty well. He was cooperative, and she was glad of it.

There were a couple of stablehands who could have untacked Major, but Lisa wanted the opportunity to work with him and get to know him. And there was no better way to learn about a horse than to take care of him.

Debbie was untacking her horse next to her. Lisa thought it was a good chance to be friendly.

"Barry's really a good teacher, isn't he?" she remarked while she removed Major's bridle.

"He's tough, if that's what you mean," Debbie said. "Sometimes I think he's too tough. You can only remember so much at one time—"

"That's not what Max thinks," Lisa said, encouraged by the girl's response. "Our instructor at home thinks you should be able to remember everything. After all, *he* does. Once, he told me eight things I was doing wrong at once!"

Debbie looked at her strangely. Probably Debbie thought that if Lisa could make so many mistakes all at once, she really wasn't worthy of riding with Debbie. Lisa decided on the spot that if that was the way Debbie felt, she really didn't want to have anything to do with her. She turned one hundred percent of her attention to Major, who needed a good brushing.

Brushing, Lisa found, was the perfect activity to do when you were angry. You grabbed the brush and scraped at the horse's coat. The angrier you were, the more vigorously you brushed, and the more your horse liked it. She could tell Major was enjoying himself.

By the time Lisa was finished, Major's coat was smooth and clean. He was ready for a drink.

Lisa led the horse to the trough at the paddock end of the barn. Fred, the stablehand, was there, holding on to three horses at once and paying attention to

none of them. It was a warm day and the horses were
still hot. They were guzzling water, which was dangerous. Overheated, overwatered horses could get bad
stomachaches.

Lisa wasn't sure what to do. She knew what Fred
was doing was wrong, but how could she tell him?
"Haven't they had enough?" she suggested.

"I don't think so," Fred said. "They're still drink-
ing."

Of course they were, but that wasn't the point. Lisa
didn't want to get into an argument with Fred, but she
would if it meant keeping the horses from illness.
Luckily Betty, the head stablehand, arrived and spoke
for her.

"Fred, those horses have had enough water for now!
Put them in the paddock and bring down a fresh bale
of hay." Fred yanked the horses back from the trough
and took them to the paddock. Lisa didn't like his
yanking, either, but at least it wasn't dangerous to the
animals.

Betty shook her head. "He's new," she confided to
Lisa. "He's the son of some friend of Barry's and he's
supposed to be this horse genius, but he isn't. He's
more work than he is help."

Still muttering to herself, Betty left to help a
camper who was having trouble loosening his horse's
girth.

One thing was certain: Stevie had been absolutely right about the stablehands—or at least one of them. The best way to make sure their horses were well taken care of was to do it themselves.

She patted Major's neck and led him to the paddock, where he would stay until she could give him some fresh hay.

In a few minutes, Fred reappeared, carrying a bale of hay on a wheelbarrow. He dumped it onto the barn floor, snapped the wire that held it, and began breaking off flakes, which were chunks of the hay, for each horse.

Lisa took a flake to feed to Major. As far as she was concerned, fresh hay had about the nicest smell in the world. She sniffed deeply.

Something was wrong. It didn't smell right. It didn't smell rotten, but it just didn't smell like fresh hay. It had an odd odor.

Carole was just entering the paddock with her horse. "What's up?" she asked, noticing the funny look on Lisa's face.

"I don't know," Lisa said. "But the hay smells funny." She held it out to Carole.

Carole felt the hay, rubbing it between her fingers. She sniffed a few strands of it and then the whole bunch of it together.

"It's moldy," Carole said. "I sure hope none of the horses have had any of this."

"Fred just brought it down from the loft. He's over—"

Lisa didn't get to finish. When horses' well-being was at stake, Carole never wasted a minute.

"Betty!" Carole called out. She ran over to Betty and showed her the hay.

Within a few minutes, Betty gathered up all the hay from the bale that Fred had brought and put it in a pile outside, well away from the barn. Moldy hay could not only make horses sick, but it could also start fires. Betty didn't want to take any chances.

She had Fred bring another bale down, and together they tested it. It was just fine. Fred cut it open and each of The Saddle Club girls took a flake for her horse. The girls had to hurry a little. There was an unmounted riding class in five minutes, followed by an instructional film before dinner. Moose Hill might have a problem with at least one stablehand, but it was serious about teaching riding skills, and the girls wouldn't have any free time until after dinner.

They jogged across the field to the rec hall, where their unmounted class was taking place.

"Saddle Club Meeting after dinner," Carole said. "We've got a lot to talk about!"

Lisa and Stevie certainly agreed with that.

"Where shall we meet?" Lisa asked.

"How about by the pond?" Stevie suggested. "There's a clearing on the shore near our cabin."

The girls agreed that it would be a nice place to be in the evening. The water, stars, and moonlight would make the perfect setting for a Saddle Club Meeting.

"OUCH!" *SLAP!* "I got it," Stevie said. "One more wretched mosquito has met his maker. And here comes another to take its place." *Slap!*

The lakeside in the evening *was* a pretty spot, and unfortunately one million mosquitoes seemed to agree.

Carole ignored Stevie's tirade against the entire insect population of western Virginia. "I can't believe these girls," she began. "I've never seen such a snotty attitude—like they're too good to ride with anybody else!"

Lisa told them about Debbie's reaction to her casual remark about Max giving her eight instructions at once. "And the boys are just as bad," she added.

"Not all of them," Stevie said. They didn't have to ask her whom she had in mind.

"Not all of the girls are awful, either," Lisa admitted. "After all, Nora is pretty nice. And that girl Lily something, who was riding the gray, seemed friendly."

"Sure, some of them are fine. I guess *most* of them are fine," Carole conceded. "But the snotty ones are unbelievable. They are so convinced they're going to win all the ribbons at the show next week just because they won them before. And that they deserve them! Ugh, I *hate* that kind of snobbishness."

"So do I," Lisa said. "So does almost everybody. But what can we do?" She slapped a mosquito. "I mean it's not as if we can change them."

"Why not?" Carole asked. "I mean why not try to change them?"

"Oooooh, look," Stevie interrupted, pointing. On the far side of the pond, the sun was setting. Above the trees, the sky was streaked with a breathtaking array of oranges, yellows, and pinks. The scene was perfectly reflected on the glasslike surface of the pond.

"Very beautiful," Lisa agreed.

"Yeah, so romantic," Stevie said dreamily.

Dreamy was not Stevie's usual state. Carole didn't think Stevie had ever noticed a sunset before in her life, but she decided to keep that observation to herself. She tossed a small pebble into the water. It made circles, rippling the sunset's reflection.

A frog croaked.

"Oh, cute!" Stevie said.

It was too much for Carole. "Cute? What's so cute about a frog?" she asked grumpily. She was getting tired of this new nature-loving phase. Stevie had the good sense not to answer.

"So how are we going to change everything?" Lisa asked, resuming their discussion.

"Oh, yes," Carole said, brightening. "The obvious way. These girls think they're going to win all the ribbons, right?"

Lisa and Stevie nodded.

"So, we don't let them. *We* win them all instead. That'll show them!"

Her friends grinned wickedly. Carole continued, "The trick is going to be letting Elsa and Debbie get overconfident—not that they're not already. Anyway, what we've got to do is to *look* like we're bumbling beginners. You know, we'll make dumb mistakes so they can feel superior. Then, when the time comes— whammo! We'll take all the blues!"

"What a fabulous idea!" Lisa laughed. "Only it's mostly going to be you two, you know—partly because you know so much and partly because Stevie will be riding Topside. I think I feel a Saddle Club project coming on. We just have to work like crazy, right? And knock their boots off!"

"Yes!" Stevie said enthusiastically, suddenly drawn into the conversation. "We can do it. I know we can!" She slapped another mosquito. "Now can we please go inside?"

"Not quite," Lisa said. "There's another problem, in case you didn't know, and his name is Fred. I heard

Betty complaining. It seems he's new and he thinks he knows a lot, but he doesn't. If you care about your horses, you'll do all the work yourself."

Carole stood up and stretched. "He's trouble all right. I guess we were all thinking we could have a vacation from hard stable work here, but it's no vacation when your horse is in danger."

"Yeah, yeah," Stevie said, obviously anxious to conclude the conversation. She slapped another mosquito vigorously. "I think I'm being eaten alive!"

"Okay, I've killed enough mosquitoes for the night too. Your wish is granted, Stevie—we can go inside," Carole said, pronouncing the meeting over.

"Not a minute too soon," Stevie said. She and Lisa stood up to go. The sun had completely set and it took them a minute to get used to the darkness of the woods. "I think it's this way." She squinted.

Then the girls heard the sound of someone rustling through the leaves. They paused, unsure of what to do.

"Hello?" a boy's voice called. "Stevie, is that you?" It was Phil.

"Oh, yes, I'm here with Carole and Lisa," she said. Lisa could hear the excitement rise in Stevie's voice.

Phil came close enough so they could all see him. "It's such a nice clear night out, I thought maybe you'd like to go for a walk?" he suggested. He was looking at all three of them, but Lisa knew he was really speaking only to Stevie.

Carole didn't seem to realize it, though. "Oh, the mosquitoes are just terrible. We're heading back to our cabin. Some other time, okay?"

"What mosquitoes?" Stevie asked.

Before Lisa and Carole knew what was happening, Stevie and Phil were off for a walk around the pond.

"Is that what love is like?" Carole asked Lisa as they returned to the cabin. "You have absolutely no sense left?"

"I don't know," Lisa said. She scratched her arm. "But I'm glad I'm not in love. Stevie's going to be awfully itchy tomorrow!"

5

IF, TWENTY-FOUR hours earlier, someone had told Stevie Lake that she would be stumbling over bushes and roots in a mosquito-infested forest on a dark night without a flashlight, she never would have believed him. Now, she was doing all those things and she wasn't even questioning her sanity. She was having too much fun.

"Here's a place we can sit," Phil said, motioning to a grassy hill that overlooked the darkened pond. They sat down facing the water and continued talking.

Stevie had never had such an easy time talking to a boy. Phil seemed to understand everything she said and it made her talk even more.

She told him about The Saddle Club and some of the things they'd done together. He loved hearing about their trip to Kate Devine's dude ranch, The Bar None. He'd been to a dude ranch once, too, and had had a great time.

"Some people who ride English are really snobby about Western riding," Stevie said. "Not me. I like riding, period. Any kind of riding. I do English riding because that's what we have in Virginia, but I'll ride any way I can because I love horses."

"Yeah, me too," Phil agreed. "But I do really enjoy the competitions in English riding, don't you?"

"I haven't been in too many shows, so maybe I'm not the best person to judge—but if the competitive mood around here is anything to go by, I don't *want* to be in a lot of shows."

Phil looked at her in surprise. "What are you talking about?"

"Oh, how about Elsa and Debbie, for starters?" she said. "You were here last year, right? From what I heard from Nora and a couple of other people, we're talking killer competition. No nice stuff about doing the best you can and learning from others. Elsa won't talk to anybody in the cabin because she's afraid we're all part of some spy ring to learn her secrets for success and Debbie is just convinced that she's better than we are—you know, like we're not good enough to share the air in her cabin?"

Phil laughed. "It doesn't take you long to figure people out, does it?" he asked. "I mean you got those two right away."

"They don't exactly keep their obnoxious personalities hidden," Stevie said. "I wonder why Barry put them in the same cabin with one another—and with *us*. I mean things are not looking good for the next two weeks."

"You aren't thinking of leaving, are you?" Phil asked quickly. "I mean, I'd hate—"

Stevie had a nice warm tingly feeling when she realized that Phil was really worried that she might go away. "No, I'm not leaving," Stevie assured him. "And neither are my friends. We've got something else in mind."

"Oh yeah?" he asked, obviously curious. "What's that?"

For a moment Stevie faltered. The Saddle Club had never talked about secrecy. Still, she wasn't sure if she should tell Phil about something the club was doing. She could definitely trust him, but would it be right to tell him without consulting her friends?

"It's sort of a Saddle Club project," she began uncertainly. "We're working on a way to give Elsa and Debbie—and anyone like them—a taste of their own medicine. It's still in the planning stages."

"Oh," Phil said. Stevie thought he sounded a little hurt not to be in on the plan.

"It's really too bad you've got those two in your cabin," Phil continued. "It gives you the wrong impression of this place. Nobody else is like that—at least not that bad. Moose Hill is a wonderful place and Barry is a great camp director and instructor. I had a neat time here last year, and I'm beginning to get the feeling that I'm going to have an even better time this year."

Stevie knew better than to ask him what he meant by that. "Tell me about Teddy," she said, changing the subject.

Phil had owned Teddy for three years. He'd had a pony before that and Teddy was his first horse. Teddy boarded at the stable where Phil rode. The Marstons didn't have room for a horse at their house.

"I offered to share my bedroom with Teddy, but Mom pointed out that the stairs could be kind of tricky."

"Boy, I'd do anything to have a horse of my own," Stevie told him. "I'd even trade one of my brothers."

"What a sacrifice!" Phil grinned. "I thought you said you'd trade one of them for a pack of bubble gum!"

"That too," Stevie agreed. "Any day. And I don't like bubble gum."

"So if Topside isn't your horse, whose is he?" Phil asked.

Stevie explained how Max had bought him from Dorothy DeSoto when she'd injured her back and had to give up competitive riding.

"That's Dorothy DeSoto's horse? You mean *the* Dorothy DeSoto?" Stevie nodded. "I'm impressed," Phil said. "With a horse like that under you, you'll probably take *all* the ribbons in the show."

"You mean you don't think I have the skill to do it by myself? I have to have a championship horse?" Stevie was a little annoyed at his tone. It made her wonder just how right he was when he'd said that Elsa and Debbie were the only two obnoxious competitors in camp.

"That's not what I meant at all," Phil reassured her. "I just meant that a rider as good as you on a horse as experienced at Topside . . . well, you may be unbeatable."

"That's the idea," Stevie said. He smiled at her.

There was a long silence then. All Stevie heard was the gentle lapping of the pond water on the shore and the occasional hum of hungry mosquitoes. She bent her legs and wrapped her arms around them, hugging them close.

"You cold?" Phil asked. "You could have my sweater."

"I'm okay."

"Well, you *look* cold," Phil remarked, removing his sweater. He put it across her shoulders and left his own arm there as well—for extra warmth, of course.

"Thanks," she said. "I guess I *was* a little chilly. I just didn't know it."

"You're welcome," he said. Then he took his other hand and reached for Stevie's chin, turning her face toward his.

Stevie couldn't believe this was happening to her. Her mind was a jumble of confused thoughts and her heart was galloping like mad. *Phil was about to kiss her!* And she'd never been kissed by a boy before in her life! She didn't know what to do. Should she close her eyes? Open them? Look away? Look up? Or just plain run?

In the faint evening light, she could see Phil smiling at her. Was he as confused as she was? He didn't seem to be. Maybe he could read all of her thoughts and was laughing at her. What an awful idea.

"It's going to be fun riding with you," Phil said, breaking the silence. "I think I'll even enjoy beating you in the horse show!" he teased.

Then he hesitated. Stevie gulped . . . and in that moment's hesitation, there came a sound. It was the sound of taps on the camp PA system. That meant they were already supposed to be in their cabins—with the lights out.

"Boy, we've got to go!" Phil said, standing up suddenly. "Barry can be pretty strict about lights out. We'll have to run."

Stevie stood up, and Phil took her hand to lead her through the woods as they hurried back to the cabin area. He seemed to know his way very well, in spite of the darkness. Within a few minutes, he'd brought her to her front door.

"See you in the morning," he whispered, waving to her.

"Yeah," she whispered back and waved.

As soon as Stevie turned to the cabin, she saw Lisa and Carole waiting for her by the screen door.

"Get in here fast!" Lisa hissed. "Nora says there's going to be a bed check in about two minutes!"

Stevie dashed up the stairs. As fast as she could, she took off her sneakers. There wasn't time to change into her pajamas before the bed check. She just climbed into the bed and pulled the sheets and blanket up high to hide her clothes.

A moment later, the cabin door opened and Betty stepped in. Stevie peeked through one squinted eye. Betty glanced around the cabin and, assured there was a camper in each of the beds, turned to leave.

"Good night, girls. Sweet dreams," Betty said.

Sweet dreams? Stevie thought. *You bet!* She was still wearing Phil's warm sweater, and she pulled it around her shoulders and snuggled down in the bed. She touched her chin where Phil had touched it. *Sweet dreams, indeed!*

6

THE HARDEST TIME of the day at camp was in the first class after lunch. It was the only class The Saddle Club had with both Debbie and Elsa. It was the class in which they had to give Debbie and Elsa the impression that they were complete idiots.

"Stevie, what's the matter with you?" Barry said in an irritated tone. "You know your diagonals as well as you know your own name!"

"Oh, but could you review it for me one more time?" Stevie whined convincingly.

Debbie and Elsa smirked.

Lisa and Carole smirked, too, but for a different reason. Stevie was doing a wonderful job convincing Debbie and Elsa that she was a dolt.

The whole class listened patiently while Barry explained diagonals to Stevie. Diagonals are related to a horse's trot. At the trot, the horse's diagonal front and back feet move together, making a two-beat gait. The rider is supposed to post, or rise and sit, with the two beats. When the horse changes directions—or reins, as it is called—the rider changes diagonals. That means that the rider sits for two beats and then begins posting again. New riders always found it a little complicated. Experienced riders did it properly, without thinking. Stevie was an experienced rider, but she was acting like the newest rider there ever was.

Elsa and Debbie gloated. The Saddle Club girls knew that the more inexperienced they appeared, the more certain Elsa and Debbie would be of victory in the horse show. Their plan was working.

Mornings were easier on them than afternoons. The girls had two classes every morning, and both were without Elsa and Debbie, so they could be as good as they wanted to be.

The first real class of the day was a jump class. Stevie and Carole had been jumping for a while and were quite good at it. Lisa had never jumped a horse intentionally. One she'd had to make a very speedy getaway from a bull in a pasture and had taken her horse over a four-foot fence. Max would have blown his stack at all three girls for being *in* the pasture with the bull in the first place and would have totally lost it if he'd learned how they'd gotten *out,* so they'd never told him about it and had sworn one another to secrecy. Also, having stayed on her horse on one jump didn't make Lisa an expert—just lucky.

While Stevie and Carole worked on perfecting style over jumps at all levels, Lisa worked with cavalettis.

Cavalettis, Lisa learned, were really just poles laid on the ground at intervals that would allow her and Major to get used to obstacles and to keep his strides even. Lisa strongly suspected that Major had a lot more experience in jumping over obstacles than she did. That was okay. Lisa was learning so quickly that she was sure she'd be jumping soon.

By the third day of working with cavalettis, Lisa found that the most important thing she had to do was to control Major's strides and to learn how long his strides were at various gaits.

"I can't believe how much fun I'm having beginning my jumping work," Lisa told her friends while they cleaned tack in between classes.

"Just wait until you really jump over something," Carole said. "There's nothing like it. When you do it, it will mean that you have a whole new kind of control over your horse and a whole new skill in your riding. Don't you agree, Stevie?"

"Oh, yes," Stevie said. "Phil and I both *love* jumping!"

Lisa and Carole exchanged glances. They were getting used to Stevie referring to herself as "Phil and I." It seemed that now that Stevie had a boyfriend, she was no longer one person, but part of a pair. It was always "Phil and I" or "Phil said" or some variation on the theme. Carole and Lisa both liked Phil, but Stevie was really carrying the "we" bit a little too far.

"Are you and Phil finished soaping the saddle?" Carole asked innocently.

The joke was lost on Stevie. "Phil? Is he here?" She turned, looking around for him.

"No, he's not actually here," Lisa said. "But you talk about him so much that he could be."

"Oh," Stevie said, blushing. Lisa would have thought that Stevie would be the last person in the world to blush, but she was doing an incredible amount of it these days.

"Do you think this is incurable?" Lisa asked Carole after Stevie had left to put Topside's clean tack away. Since they'd spotted Phil headed in the general direction of the tack room, the girls didn't think they'd see either of them until lunchtime, when they'd be flooded with new sentences beginning with "Phil and I" and "Stevie and I." It was strange to see an independent girl like Stevie become so immersed in another person.

"I don't know," Carole answered. "But it's hard to

imagine good old Stevie going through the rest of her life in a haze."

"That makes sense," Lisa said as she buffed the last square inch of Major's saddle. "Good old Stevie is still there, under all those "Phil and I's" and blushes. She'll reemerge soon enough. Then maybe we'll be wishing for the dreamy Stevie again."

"Not me," Carole declared. "Barry had to call Stevie's turn three times this morning in class. She was too busy helping Phil untangle his reins!"

Lisa laughed. "Enough! I'm putting my saddle away and then I'm going to check on Major. He had a stone in his shoe today and I want to make sure it's not still tender. See you at lunch." She walked over to the tack room.

Somebody had put a saddle where Major's belonged. Lisa didn't know whose saddle it was, but she had a good idea whose mistake it was, and his name was Fred. There were several empty saddle racks. Lisa moved the saddle to one of them and put Major's in its proper place. She looked around. A lot of the saddles were carelessly balanced on their racks. Lisa shifted them so they all sat straight and, frowning at Fred's carelessness, left the tack room.

Major was in his own stall in the lower section of the barn. She wanted to keep an eye on him until she was sure his foot was all right. Most of the time, when a horse had a stone stuck in his shoe any tenderness disappeared as soon as the stone was removed. Lisa was just being cautious, because every once in a while a stone could cause trouble that continued after it was removed.

Lisa clipped a lead to Major's halter and led him out into the open area. She walked him the length of the barn. He seemed fine, just as she'd expected. She returned him to the stall and closed the gate.

Basil, Carole's horse, had the stall next to Major's. Lisa checked on him as well. He was fine. But there was something wrong with the horse next to Basil. It was Alamo, Nora's horse. Lisa knew that Nora had finished class over an hour earlier, but the horse still had his saddle and bridle on. Nora wouldn't be riding him for at least another hour, so there was no need for him to be tacked up while he was supposed to be resting in the stall.

Fred again.

Lisa considered the possibility that Alamo was going out again so soon that leaving the tack on was intentional. However, the last time she'd seen Nora, the girl was dismounting and handing the reins to Fred, and Lisa remembered distinctly that Nora had said she was going to take a swim before lunch. No, there was nothing intentional about this—it was just laziness. Lisa did what had to be done. She brought Alamo out of the stall, removed his saddle and bridle, put him back in, and took the tack up to the tack room.

When she'd finished putting Alamo's tack away, she found Betty in her office. Lisa didn't like tattling, but the horses' welfare was at stake here. It mattered.

She told Betty about the mess in the tack room and about Alamo's tack being left on him. Betty didn't say much besides "Hmmm," but her lips set into a thin angry line and she glared.

"Thanks," Betty said, dismissing Lisa.

Lisa didn't know what that meant. Probably Betty didn't like tattling any more than she did. It was a rotten thing to do, but at any stable, horses came first.

BY THE FOURTH day of camp, the girls were so well settled in that they felt like they'd been there forever. Stevie and Carole were getting good at being bad, Lisa was getting better at being good, and they were all having a wonderful time. While Lisa and Carole's favorite class was jumping and Stevie's favorite was whichever one she had with Phil, they all agreed that they liked their early-morning trail rides the best. Anybody who wanted to could join in. Others were expected to use the time to work on specific skills in the ring. The trail ride came before breakfast, when the sun was just up and the fields were still dewy. It was an informal ride, one without constant reminders about keeping heels down and toes in, shoulders back or chin up. It was just for fun, and it was *lots* of fun.

"Sitting trot and then canter!" Eleanor called from her lead position. At the sound of her words, the horses came to life, ready to do what their riders wanted, ready to follow Eleanor's instruction.

Max always told his riders that horses couldn't speak English, so they had to use their hands, legs, and seat to communicate. Lisa suspected that wasn't entirely correct. Most horses she'd ridden seemed to know the words for the gaits. As soon as Eleanor called out the word "trot," Major was trotting. It didn't take much longer until he was cantering.

Cantering was wonderful. It was sort of a rocking gait, and Lisa slid forward and back slightly in the saddle with Major's strides. Although it was much faster than the trot, it was smoother and Lisa felt more secure. Major seemed to feel her excitement and responded with both greater power and smoothness. Lisa couldn't help herself. She grinned with the pleasure of the experience.

Eleanor's hand went up and the riders slowed their horses to a trot and then, quickly, to a walk. Carole pulled up beside Lisa.

"It's wonderful, isn't it?" Carole asked.

Lisa nodded.

"It's what riding is about, you know. I don't mean

just cantering. A horse shouldn't be asked to canter too much. What I mean is—"

"I know," Lisa said. "Riding is about having fun, and this is as much fun as there is, right?"

Carole smiled at her friend. Sometimes she couldn't believe how much Lisa had learned about riding in just a few short months. Lisa was good already, and she was going to get a lot better as time went on.

"That's one of the things I was going to say, but there's something else, too. The thing about riding is both learning enough to have fun, like we are right now, and then having enough fun to learn, like we do in class. The more you know, the better you ride, and the more fun it is."

The trail was narrowing, so Lisa dropped back behind Carole in line. "You mean that one day I'll enjoy this even more?" she asked.

"Absolutely!" Carole called over her shoulder.

Lisa sighed contentedly. There was a *lot* to look forward to!

AT LUNCH THAT day, Lisa found that there was even more to look forward to.

"Girls and boys, may I have your attention, please," Barry said, standing up in front of the group as they began eating their tuna fish sandwiches.

"Oh, this is going to be our surprise event," Phil

said, leaning toward Stevie and her friends to explain. "Barry does something special at the end of the first week of every session. Last year, we went to see Combined Training at a nearby stable. That would be great—"

"And this year, I have planned something entirely different," Barry was saying. "Tomorrow morning after breakfast, we are leaving on an overnight camping trip. We will return the following afternoon. Please make sure that all your horses are in shape for the trip and that you have—"

Barry went on. He had a nearly endless list of things they had to do before they could go. The girls remembered their last overnight, right after Lisa had come to Pine Hollow and started riding. It had been fantastic, and they were sure this one would be, too.

"Give me a break!" somebody growled. It was Debbie.

"What's the matter with an overnight trip?" Carole wanted to know.

Debbie made an unbelievably rude face. "Overnight? When we've got a show to train for? The next thing you know, he'll have us doing—"

"Mounted games!" Barry announced. "Tomorrow after dinner when it's still light, we'll set up teams and have a sort of mini-gymkhana!"

Many campers clapped with delight. Debbie didn't.

Neither did Elsa. The Saddle Club girls didn't care what those two sourpusses thought. They'd been working hard on their skills and it would be fun to put them to the test with some games.

Lisa remembered what Carole had said to her on the morning trail ride. It seemed that her prediction was already coming true!

CAROLE TIGHTENED BASIL'S girth and checked the stirrup length. In general, stirrups were the right length for a rider if they were about the length of the rider's arm. Nobody but Carole should have used Basil's saddle, but she could tell at a glance that somebody had fiddled with her stirrups. *Fred again,* she told herself, shortening the leather by two buckle holes.

Carole actually wasn't sorry she had to fuss with saddle adjustments, because right on Basil's other side, a drama was unfolding. As long as she had an excuse to be where she was, she could get an earful.

"I'm just not feeling very well, Barry," Debbie whined. Carole, reaching under Basil to needlessly straighten the girth, saw a phony pained look on Debbie's face.

"Well, *where* aren't you feeling well?" Barry asked impatiently.

"Oh, sort of here," she said, gesturing vaguely toward her entire body. Carole thought that was even more fake than her last statement.

"Have you seen the nurse?" Barry asked.

"No, but I've had this happen before," Debbie said. "It'll be all better in a day or so."

Carole didn't think there was anything Barry could do about Debbie's mysterious stomachache and apparently he agreed. He told Debbie to take her gear back to the cabin. She could stay in the camp until they got back from the trip. Carole could see the pleased look on Debbie's face as she returned to Cabin Three. She'd bet a stirrup to a saddle that Debbie's vague ailment would be cleared up within the hour and she'd be on her horse, in the ring, practicing for the horse show all alone, all day.

Or would Debbie be all alone?

"Barry, can I talk to you?" It was Elsa. It turned out that she had a strange pain in her right ear. Elsa said she didn't think it was serious, but she could remember one time when she'd had an ache very much like this one and within a few hours, she'd been horribly sick, so she thought maybe it wouldn't be a good idea to go on the camping trip, and didn't Barry agree?

Barry didn't agree. The tone of his voice made it

clear to Carole that he'd had about enough games from Elsa and Debbie. On the other hand, Carole suspected that Barry would decide to let Elsa stay in camp because she and Debbie deserved one another and the rest of the campers deserved a vacation from them.

As Carole figured, Barry told Elsa she could stay at camp. Like Debbie, Elsa was grinning victoriously as she returned to the cabin. Carole would have loved to see their faces when each discovered that the other had wangled her way out of the camping trip.

Finally satisfied with her stirrup length, Carole lowered the flap of her saddle, secured her pack, and mounted up. It was time to hit the trail.

She turned around in her saddle, looking for her friends. She couldn't wait to share the wonderful news about Debbie and Elsa.

"MORE THAN TWENTY-FOUR hours of trail riding—isn't it fabulous!" Lisa said to Carole as they proceeded through a woody area.

"Especially without the Miss Uncongeniality Award winners," Carole agreed.

"Only trouble is that I'm missing a jump class," Lisa remarked.

Carole's eyes lit up. That meant she had an idea. One of her favorite things to do was to share her riding knowledge with her friends, and most of the time, they welcomed it. If this was going to be a way to learn jumping on a trail ride, Lisa was willing to listen.

"Try this," Carole told her friend. "I think Barry's about to start us trotting. You can do it in jump position. It's not the same as working with cavaletti, but it's important."

Of course, Lisa thought. Eleanor, the jump instructor, kept stressing the necessity of a good jump position. In jump position, the rider's seat was slightly raised, and you leaned forward with your back parallel to the horse's neck. It was the position a rider needed to go over a jump, remain balanced, and absorb the impact of landing with the knees. It was critical to have a good jump position, so it was important to practice as much as possible. Lisa rose slightly, leaned forward, and kept her hands still at the horse's neck.

"Good job," Carole said. "Remember to keep your toes up and your hands steady."

At the front, Barry raised his hand to signal a change of pace. In seconds, they were all trotting. Much to Lisa's surprise, the other campers were following her lead and trotting in jump position. It seemed that even without the presence of Debbie and Elsa, the riders were competitive. Nobody wanted anybody to practice anything more than anybody else. Lisa didn't know whether to laugh or be sad. Since Carole was right there, they exchanged looks and laughed. It was better than being sad.

When they finished the trot and were walking again, Carole continued instructing Lisa. Carole was a natural teacher. She knew a lot about horses and riding and she liked to share it. Sometimes her friends got a little tired of it, but this time, two things kept Lisa from stopping her. The first was that everything Carole was telling her was absolutely right. The second was that every rider within earshot was hanging on to Carole's every word. It was not just funny, it was hilarious.

Stevie, who was riding next to Phil, was close enough to see what was going on. Lisa spotted the familiar mischievous grin on her friend's face and knew something good was coming.

"Hey, Carole!" Stevie called, spurring the horse toward her best friends. "Is Lisa having trouble with her form again? Let *me* help!"

When Stevie arrived, the fun began. She told Carole to ride on the other side so they could both watch Lisa, but she really meant so they could watch the other riders. Then Stevie started barking instructions, and they were all wrong. The eavesdroppers followed every word she said. Within a few minutes, Stevie had them all riding sitting on the back edges of their saddles, arms fully extended at shoulder height, legs straight and stretched forward.

Barry turned to check on his riders. He was completely astonished to see all of them, except The Saddle Club, posed like zombies on horseback!

"Halloween requires costumes and your horses require proper riders!" he snapped. "All of you! Back in position! We're going to canter!"

Lisa hoped that the sound of his horse's hooves covered the burst of giggles from The Saddle Club.

"What was that all about?" Phil asked Stevie when she returned to his side.

"Just a little joke," she said, embarrassed. After all, Phil had followed her silly instructions, too.

"What kind of joke?" he persisted.

"It's all this dumb competition," she began. "Even without Elsa and Debbie, it's like everybody's spying. I just thought I'd give them something for their trouble. It was pretty funny, you know."

"To you, maybe," Phil said.

That was all he said for a while. Stevie didn't like the idea that she'd made him feel foolish, but, she reasoned, he'd been acting stupid by following her directions.

After what seemed a long time, but was really no more than five minutes, he made a peace offering. "I brought some marshmallows," he said. "Want to sneak out of camp after lights out and have a little picnic of our own?"

Stevie grinned and nodded. "Yeah, I'd like that," she said, glad that his feelings weren't still hurt.

WHEN THEY REACHED the campsite, The Saddle Club girls knew just what to do. The rule on the Pine Hollow trip was horses first, riders second. They dismounted and untacked their horses and led them to the nearby stream, where they could get a drink of water. Then the horses would need grooming and fresh hay, followed by more water and, finally, a full meal of grain, which had been delivered to the campsite's paddock. After that, the girls would check their tack and stow it for the night. Then it would be time to set up the campsite.

It was that simple—and it was that complicated.

"I can't lift the saddle."

"*I've* got to have something to eat first."

"I don't know how to do this stuff."

"Why can't Fred do it?"

"I thought we were supposed to learn to ride, not work!"

And so on. The Saddle Club couldn't believe the way some of the campers were acting. Some of them made honest attempts to complete the obvious chores like untacking, but a lot of them seemed to think that everything except the actual riding was beneath them.

Stevie, Carole, and Lisa were too well trained by

Max. Nothing having to do with stable management and horse care was beneath a good rider. Patiently, the girls pitched in to help other campers complete the work. It didn't earn them many thanks. Mostly what they got were surprised looks.

Carole helped the others with untacking, Lisa managed the watering and feeding, and Stevie supervised grooming. Stevie, it turned out, was the all-time champion hoof-picker.

"Three stones!" she announced proudly as the third pebble in one horse's hoof hit the ground. Her friends applauded. The other campers remained mystified.

When Fred delivered the first bale of hay to the paddock area, Lisa snapped the wire that held it and began breaking it into one-horse flakes. But something was wrong, and she knew what it was right away. The hay had that same odd, almost sickly sweet smell that she'd noticed in the moldy bale back at camp.

"Fred, this stuff doesn't smell right to me," she said. Fred shrugged and walked away.

Lisa couldn't feed that hay to the horses. It would almost certainly make them sick. One horse with colic was bad news, but a whole paddock full of them would be a disaster. She got one of the boys to give her a hand. Together they carried the moldy bale into an open area of the woods and spread it around on the forest floor, where it would eventually dry out and where no horses could reach it. Then they found a fresh bale, which they opened and fed to the horses in the makeshift paddock.

Barry and Betty were busy overseeing the mixing of the horse's grain. Lisa didn't want to bother them about Fred's most recent mistake. Besides, she wasn't too sure it was her place to tell them. After all, no harm had been done. She told herself she'd think about it later. Her thoughts were interrupted by more squabbling campers.

"I'll tell you one thing. I don't care *what* Barry said. I'm not picking up kindling for every single fireplace in the whole campsite. I'm not sitting at every fire, so I'm not building every fire!"

"Me, neither!" said the girl's companion.

Well, at least there were two campers who agreed on something!

Lisa returned to the campsite and helped pitch tents. Carole, being a Marine Corps brat, was of course the champion at that. Finally, the campers finished their chores. At last they could enjoy the campsite.

It was a nice campsite, with tents pitched among tall pine trees. Carole like camping in piny woods, because the pine needles cushioned the ground and that was good for sleeping. The area was open enough so that there was no danger from the camp fires. Leaning against neighboring tree trunks, Carole and her friends could see the clear sky above. It was still light. They were having an early dinner, so there would still be plenty of light for their mounted games.

"This sort of reminds me of the story of The Little Red Hen," Carole remarked to her friends, taking her first bite of Trail Stew and washing it down with fruit punch. "Nobody wants to share the work, but everybody wants to share the cake."

Stevie and Lisa agreed totally.

"Even Phil seems to catch the disease sometimes," Stevie remarked, surprising Lisa and Carole with her frankness.

The girls ate the rest of their meal in silence. For one thing, they were really tired, too tired to do their usual chatting. For another, right then, there didn't seem to be anything to say. It had all been said and it was trouble and they all knew it.

THE FIRST GAME Barry chose for them to play was Follow-the-Leader. He very wisely chose Stevie as a leader. Nobody was more able to do so many ridiculous things on horseback. The only problem was that the first thing Stevie did as leader was to imitate the silly position she'd gotten everybody into on the afternoon ride. Both Carole and Lisa were laughing so hard that they couldn't do it.

"You two, you're out!" Barry yelled.

They pulled over to the side and watched the rest. Stevie had the riders sit both cross-legged and backwards on their saddles—horses standing still, of course. She tried a sidesaddle seat, but it was difficult without a genuine sidesaddle, and she almost fell off

73

herself. When Phil and another rider did, they joined Carole and Lisa on the sidelines.

At the end of the game, Barry took over and started them on Simon-Says. Lisa and Carole thought Stevie had done more amusing things, but it didn't matter. It was all fun.

Next, they played a game called Touch Wood. It was sort of like tag, but anybody touching wood—for example, a tree, a fence post, or a gate—was safe. But every time the whistle blew, everybody had to change trees or whatever wood they were touching.

"This is wild!" Lisa gasped, swapping trees with Carole at a canter while Nora chased both of them.

"And a good learning experience, too!" Carole said, reaching as long and hard as she could for her new tree, but she wasn't fast enough.

"You're It!" Nora declared.

Watching Carole, Lisa thought about what she'd said about learning. It was true. The game was great practice in horse control, particularly direction changes. Fortunately for Carole, she was a good enough rider that she wasn't It for long. Within a very short time, Lisa was It.

I'm learning, I'm learning, she told herself as she dashed after the riders who scattered across the field. *I'm learning. And most of all, I'm having fun!*

After Touch Wood, they played another variation,

Freeze Tag, which involved even more horse control than Touch Wood, since anybody who had been tagged had to remain completely still—as did the horse.

The riders concentrated so hard on their games that they barely noticed when the sun set and night came on.

"Time to quit," Barry announced. "All of you walk your horses until he's cooled down, untack him, and give him water and fresh hay. We'll meet at the camp fire in half an hour for ghost stories. Anybody who wants to can tell a ghost story, but the principle character in the story *must* be a horse!"

Contented and tired and looking forward to a quiet camp-fire time, Carole quickly took care of Basil and then helped Lisa finish putting away Major's tack.

"Wait until Barry hears the one about the werehorse!" Carole said to Lisa.

"That sounds like a Stevie kind of story," Lisa remarked.

"Yes, it does," Carole said. "And speaking of Stevie, I haven't seen her for a while, have you?"

Lisa hung Major's bridle over his saddle. "Yes, actually, I did see her—or at least the back of her. I think she and Phil are going to miss your story about the werehorse. I also think we may have to cover for her."

"What are friends for?" Carole asked. She gave

Basil a final pat on his nose. Then she turned to Lisa and slung her arm across her friend's shoulder. "Okay, so now this werehorse makes friends with a vamp-mare . . ."

STEVIE WONDERED IF she would ever get used to the feeling of Phil holding her hand when they walked. It wasn't a very efficient way to walk through a wooded area—single file was much better—but it was more fun.

"Did you bring the marshmallows?" Phil asked.

"Oh, no, I forgot. How dumb of me!"

"That's okay. After that dinner, I'm not very hungry."

"Me, neither," Stevie said. "Maybe that's why I forgot the marshmallows. You know, I really didn't want them, but I didn't know it."

Phil smiled. It was that smile that made Stevie's knees melt. "Why don't we sit down someplace?" she suggested, hoping she could sit down before she fell down. Not that his smile could really make her faint, but a full day of riding hadn't helped her knees, either.

"Here's a clearing, I think," Phil said. It was awfully hard to see. The night sky was overcast and they were deep in a forest, but there appeared to be a small open space. Carefully, Stevie lowered herself onto the crunchy leaves, sitting cross-legged. Phil sat facing her and took her hand. She no longer shivered when he did that, but she did tingle.

"Tired?" he asked.

"A little," she conceded. "I like riding and I like doing a lot of it, but Barry's schedule for us is really rugged."

"Too much for the famed Saddle Club?" Phil teased.

Stevie wasn't crazy about his tone. Phil was very special to her, but so was The Saddle Club, and she didn't like him making fun of it.

"The Saddle Club is made up of me and my two best friends," Stevie said, knowing she sounded defensive. "We've accomplished some pretty good things together in the past, and I think you'll have a chance to see us do impressive things in the future, too."

"I will?" Phil said, obviously curious.

"Yes, you will," Stevie assured him. "In fact, in case you didn't know it, we're working on several projects at this very minute!"

"Here, with me?"

"No, I don't mean here. I just mean we're in the process. It has to do with riding and it has to do with the show next weekend and it has to do with some of the campers who think they are going to win absolutely everything at the show."

"You mean like me?"

"Huh?" Stevie responded in surprise. "You mean *you* think you're going to take all the prizes?"

"Is there anybody here good enough to beat me?" Phil asked.

Stevie thought about it for a minute. It was too dark to see Phil's face, but it certainly sounded to her as if he were completely serious. It had never really occurred to her that Phil might feel that way. He was a good enough rider—experienced, secure—but a champion? No, she was better than he was.

"I'm asking," Phil repeated. "Do you think you and your friends can beat me?"

One of Stevie's biggest faults was that she often spoke before she thought.

"Of course we can beat you," she said, absolutely certain that she was one hundred percent right.

"That's what you think." He spoke sharply. Stevie was angry. How could he possibly think that he was as good a rider as she was? He was *almost* as good as she was, but not better, and certainly not better than Carole.

"You're crazy," she snapped. "The Saddle Club is going to outride, outrun, and outribbon every single rider in this camp. You included."

Stevie stood up. Phil stood up, too.

"I—" he began. Stevie didn't let him finish. She didn't want to hear whatever it was that he had to say. If he thought he was better than she was, well then he could just spend some time alone with that wonderful thought.

"I'll see you in the morning," she announced. She spun on her heel and marched through the woods. Branches snapped in her face, but she didn't feel them. She nearly tripped over a root, and didn't notice. A briar ripped at her sweater. She didn't care. For a second, she thought that she heard Phil call her name.

"Better than I am? No way!" she said to herself. "Better than Carole? Out of the question!" She continued talking as she stormed through the forest.

The woods were unfamiliar, but she remembered that the campsite was in a valley and that she and Phil had been walking uphill all the way. In just a few minutes, she came upon the flickering flames of the campsite. Unnoticed, she slipped into the tent she shared with Carole and Lisa. She put on her pajamas and climbed into her sleeping bag. She was still too angry to sleep, though.

Outside, beyond the canvas walls of her tent, she could hear her friends talking.

". . . And then the werehorse said to the vampmare, 'Don't worry, my bark is worse than my bite.' And the vampmare replied, 'That's funny— mine isn't!'" There were giggles and laughter. Stevie didn't laugh. Right then, nothing was funny, except maybe the idea that Phil-the-super-duper-rider who thought he could take all the prizes might, just might, get lost in the woods.

And *that* was a comforting notion to go to sleep by, Stevie thought, drifting off at last.

9

"Do I DETECT trouble in paradise?" Lisa asked Stevie as casually as she could manage. She was riding next to Stevie as the campers returned to Moose Hill and for the first time in days, Phil was not in sight.

"Why would you say that?" Stevie retorted.

"Maybe it has something to do with the stony look on your face," Carole said. "Which, I might add, perfectly matches the one on a certain guy's, although you might not know it, since you haven't looked at him all day."

"Who?" Stevie asked innocently. Her friends got the message.

"Well, well!" Lisa said lightly. "Looks like the old Stevie is back!"

Stevie just glared. It was clear that she wasn't up for

any teasing. Lisa and Carole decided to leave her alone.

For Lisa, it was a little sad to be returning to Moose Hill. She'd had a wonderful time on the trip, enjoying every minute of it and learning every minute of it, too, thanks to Carole.

"Since we missed jump class again today," Lisa said, "would you be able to work with me on the cavalettis and low jumps during free time this evening?"

"Oh, sure," Carole replied enthusiastically. She was as glad for an opportunity to teach as Lisa was eager for one to learn. "You know, I think you'll have a good shot at earning a ribbon in the Beginning Jumper category at the show. Don't you agree, Stevie?" Carole asked.

"I don't want to talk about the show," Stevie grumbled.

Carole and Lisa were surprised. Whatever it was that was wrong with Stevie, it wasn't just Phil. And it was clear that until Stevie got into a talking mood, they weren't going to learn a thing. In the meantime, the best thing to do was to stay out of her way.

LISA HAD HAD a vague hope that the enjoyable time the campers had shared at the campsite, with the mounted games and the silly ghost stories, might improve the general attitude around camp and make a change in the way campers took care of their horses when they returned to camp. She was wrong.

The horses had no sooner reached the barn than the campers were nearly shoving one another aside to find the best untacking position, which was nearest the tack room and required the shortest walk carrying tack. Everybody seemed grumpy and selfish. Nobody wanted to do their own work, much less help others. It wasn't the way riding should be, Lisa thought angrily. Friends helped one another and had fun working together. At least that was what she had found in The Saddle Club. So why couldn't everybody see that? Why couldn't everybody cooperate?

The whole operation was complicated by the fact that the farrier was coming in the morning. Barry had made an announcement about it. Most horses needed new shoes about once a month. A couple of the camp horses needed shoes and Barry wanted to make sure everybody who needed them would get them. All of the campers were to make a special check of their horses' hooves and shoes, and any horse who needed new shoes would be kept in a stall in the barn overnight. The farrier would arrive at dawn and most of the horses would have their shoes by noon.

Lisa finished untacking Major, got him a bucket of fresh water, and led him out by the paddock, where she could groom him in the sunlight.

Every grooming began with a check of the horse's hooves. Lisa began with Major's left front foot. There was a lot of dirt lodged in there, but it all came out with a simple picking. She tapped the shoe. It was secure. One down, three to go. His left hind foot wasn't so easy. The mud came out, but as soon as she tapped the shoe with the pick, it dropped off. That meant that Major would have to spend the night in the barn, waiting for the farrier. Worse still, he might not have his new shoes in time for her jump class. Lisa sighed. If riding horses meant having a wonderful time, it also meant learning patience.

Major's right front shoe was missing and had to be replaced. If one was gone, all four had to go, because it meant the other three might go as well. There was no getting away from it: Major needed new shoes. And in the meantime, Lisa really shouldn't ride him. She hoped Carole would let her ride Basil when they practiced this evening.

Lisa finished grooming Major, packed up his grooming gear, and took him into the stable area beneath the main barn. As she was giving him fresh hay in his stall, she suddenly remembered that she'd wanted to tell Barry about the moldy hay Fred had brought on the trip. She finished her work with Major and returned to the main level of the barn.

Barry was there, all right, but he was very busy.

Debbie, it seemed, was now completely recovered from whatever it was that she'd been sick with yesterday and was having a heated argument with Barry.

"You said the judging at the show would be fair!" Debbie said hotly.

"And it will be," Barry replied, trying to sound calm.

"How can it be fair if one of the other rider's *mother* is a judge?" Debbie challenged.

"She's a good judge," Barry said. "She's judged all kinds of competitions, including American Horse Show Association shows."

The more Lisa listened, the more she learned. It turned out that one of the judges was Elsa's mother. No wonder Debbie was so upset! It might even make her *really* sick! It occurred to Lisa that if Elsa's mother was going to judge the show, it might not be too wonderful for The Saddle Club's latest project, either, but she quickly dismissed the thought. She would love it if The Saddle Club could take all the ribbons at the show and teach some people lessons, but as she'd learned from Carole, the most important part about riding was learning enough to have fun.

In any case, it was clear that this was no time to talk to Barry, and Eleanor was nowhere in sight. That meant it was time for her to unpack her own overnight sack, put on a bathing suit, and test the waters in the pond. Without regret, she left the barn.

"STEVIE?"

Stevie didn't look up. She was working on Topside's coat, grooming it to a wonderful sheen. She knew who was talking to her. She didn't want to talk to him.

"You there?" Phil asked.

"Hmmm."

"Teddy's favoring one of his legs. He won't let me touch it. Can you help him?"

That put Stevie in a quandary. She was still steaming mad at Phil and she didn't want to lift a finger to help him. But helping Teddy was another matter. It was unfair to make Teddy suffer just because she was mad at his owner. Besides, since Phil had put it in terms of helping Teddy, she decided she could do it.

"You're the best there is at picking out stones. That's what I think it is. I hope—"

"Let's see," Stevie said abruptly. She put down the tools and looked up for the first time. Phil had cross-tied Teddy right across the barn from Topside. It was almost true that she hadn't noticed Phil until he had spoken.

She rummaged through her tool bucket, took out her own hoof pick, and walked over to the horse.

Stevie could see right away that Teddy's left front foot was bothering him. A horse at rest might lift a rear foot and casually shift his weight or just point the toe, holding the heel of the rear foot off the ground. But, when a front foot was held that way for a long time, there was probably something wrong.

Stevie approached Teddy. She patted him and spoke to him reassuringly. The last thing she wanted to do was to startle a horse with a sore foot.

"He was okay when I was riding him. I'm sure I would have noticed. So he must have just picked up a stone on the way into the barn. Isn't that strange?"

Stevie just grunted. She spoke gently to the horse. "It's okay, boy. I'm not going to hurt you. No trouble; here, boy. Just let me have a look."

She slid her hand down his leg, put her shoulder against his, and reached for the hoof. Teddy lifted it for her.

"How do you *do* that?" Phil asked. Stevie didn't bother to answer. After all, if Phil thought he was such a hotshot on horseback, why should he need any horse-care tips from her?

Gently, she probed the tissue of the hoof, removing dirt with her pick. She didn't see anything wrong right away, but as she tapped the shoe, she knew there was something in there, because Teddy flinched at the touch.

She kept talking to him. It was the best way she knew to calm a horse, and this one needed calming. So did his owner, but Stevie didn't speak to Phil.

"You picked something up here, didn't you, boy?" She felt under the shoe with the pick. "I feel something there. We'll get it out." Whatever it was, it wouldn't budge with the pick. Stevie tried the next best thing—her finger. She probed until she could reach the stone and then, slowly and carefully, began moving it. Every time it moved, Teddy reacted. Although she didn't like hurting him, it would hurt him a lot worse if she didn't get it out.

"It's coming now, boy. It'll just be a little bit longer. Hold on there, okay?"

With a final tug, Stevie got the stone out. It clattered to the barn floor. Stevie picked it up to examine it.

"That's a nasty one, boy," she told Teddy, looking at the sharply pointed stone that had been giving him so much trouble. "I don't know how you stood it at all. Now let me have another look at that hoof."

There was a bucket of water nearby. Stevie took her water brush, dipped it in the bucket, and began washing the sole of the horse's foot. When the area was clean, she could see some discoloration. "Looks like you've got a bruise here, boy," she said to Teddy. "It may be nothing, but if I were you, I'd tell my owner that I should stay in the barn tonight and be checked by the farrier in the morning. Besides, you don't want to go running all over the paddock competing with those other horses when you've got a sore foot now, do you?"

She put the horse's hoof down and stood up. "That's a good boy," she said, patting him.

"Thank you, Stevie," Phil said. "You're the best at that."

"I'm glad to know you think I'm the best at something!" Stevie retorted and, without another word, returned to grooming Topside.

She thought Phil Marston had a lot of nerve trying to make her feel better by saying she was good at getting stones out. She *was* good at it, but it wasn't what she wanted to hear him say.

When she finished with Topside, she turned him out into the paddock with the other horses and she returned to the cabin. Lisa had said something about a swim before supper. That would be good—especially if there were no boys there.

10

LISA WAS HAVING a wonderful dream. It was all about the camp-out—the trail ride, the games, the ghost stories around the camp fire. She was listening to more ghost stories around the camp fire. She could almost smell the pungent smoke. It tickled her nostrils and irritated her eyes. She was roasting marshmallows. But there was no smell of marshmallows. There was just the smell of smoke.

Lisa sat upright in bed. There was *still* a smell of smoke. "Fire!" she whispered, almost too frightened to say it out loud.

"Hmph," rumbled one of her sleeping cabin mates.

She sniffed again. There was no doubt about it. Something was burning and Lisa had the awful feeling it wasn't a camp fire. She hopped out of her bed and ran to the window. She could see the barn at the top of the hill. A flicker of orange was coming from the hay-loft.

"*FIRE!*" Lisa yelled. Everybody was awake at once.

The girls didn't wait to dress. They ran out of their cabin, screaming out the frightening word *fire* as they rushed through the cabin area. Other campers quickly joined them.

Lisa raced up the hill, Carole and Stevie beside her.

"It's the hay," Lisa said. "I know it's the hay! All that moldy hay, and Fred left it in the barn. It started a fire!"

"Come on," Carole urged. "Right now, that's not important. Someone's told Barry. He'll call the Fire Department and they'll take care of the barn. We've got to help the horses!"

The Saddle Club knew they only had a few minutes and every second could mean a horse's life! Barns were filled with things that burned well. Hay, grain, straw, dry wood—all of it would fuel the fire, and within a short time the whole thing could just about explode.

Carole pointed to the upper paddock on the far side of the barn, where the horses were beginning to panic. The horses clustered near the barn, as if they were looking for the safety of a familiar shelter. They shifted and pranced, nudging and frightening one another. Their ears were pinned back in fear and tension, their eyes were opened wide, showing white all around. The horses were in terrible danger and every instinct they had was putting them at greater risk.

"Get them away from the barn!" Carole cried. "It could collapse on them!"

Lisa saw at once that she was right. If the animals could be moved to the other end of the large paddock and kept there, they'd be safe no matter what happened to the barn. Cooped in the paddock next to the barn, they only terrified one another, endangering themselves even more. But what could the girls do?

"The hilltop!" Lisa cried to Carole. "If we can get them on the other side of the hill, they won't see the fire, and maybe they'll stay away."

Carole nodded. There wasn't a second to spare on conversation. She barked orders at everybody nearby, and everybody began following them.

"Lisa, Debbie! Climb the fence on our side—don't go inside, the horses could crush you—and try shooing them away from the barn. Jack, Nora, Elsa, go get cavalettis, jumps, barrels, anything you can think of to create a makeshift fence to restrain the horses in the far end of the paddock. You four, bring water, hay, grain, anything you can lay your hands on, to give the horses when they get there. We'll need a big welcoming committee to make them feel at home. Seth, you help Lisa and Debbie. Use your shirt to wave at them if you want. Anything to get them to move, because I've got the feeling that wall's going to collapse. And when it does, the horses aren't the only ones who will have to be out of its way!"

Lisa looked over her shoulder at the barn. The long upright slats of wood were glowing red with the heat and licking flames were visible behind them. The hay in the loft was burning so fast that the entire barn could be gone in just a few minutes. She began waving her arms at the frightened horses, just as Carole had told her. It was hard to imagine that this frantic herd of horses, prancing, jumping, and whinnying with fear, were the same horses who had been so obedient just a few hours ago when they'd been ridden. Her eyes searched among them for her own horse. But she didn't see him. Maybe he was smarter than the others. Maybe he was already safe at the far end of the field.

Then the realization hit her. Major wasn't safe in the field. He wasn't safe at all. *Major was in the barn!*

STEVIE RAN TO the lower entrance of the barn where the horses were stabled. The fire had started in the loft, at the top of the barn. "Hot air rises," she told herself. "It'll burn, the whole thing will burn, but it goes up faster than it comes down. I've got time. I've got time."

But when she got to the barn, she wasn't so certain.

The air was filled with the sound of crackling fire and it was close, too close. She could barely breathe, but the only thought she had was for the horses. Especially one horse—Teddy. She had put him in the barn, and she would get him out. There wasn't time to get Barry or Eleanor to help. All she had to do, she told herself, was to open the door. The horses would run.

She could hear their loud whinnies and cries above the terrifying crackling of the consuming fire. The horses stomped on the wood floor in complete panic, drumming their hooves irregularly.

The she heard one cry, louder than the rest. She couldn't wait. She had to free the horses. It didn't matter where they went. It just mattered that they didn't stay.

Without another thought, Stevie grabbed the handle to the door and pulled.

Nearly fifty horses pressed forward in the upper paddock toward the barn. The fence was strong, but it wasn't designed to withstand pressure like that. Lisa could feel the wood wobbling under the crush of the horses' power. She waved frantically at the animals, but it was as if they didn't see her at all. They pushed her hands away with their noses. Debbie, next to Lisa, wasn't having any more luck. Eleanor and Betty joined them, as did six other campers. Finally, with so many people trying to get them to move away, the horses stepped back, but the horses in the rear hadn't gotten the message. They pushed the whole herd forward again, surging against the weakened fence.

Lisa looked around, thinking furiously. They needed something really visible, something that would be impossible for the horses not to notice. She spotted a small stack of rags by the spigot that were used to dry the horses after their baths.

In a flash, she hopped down from the fence, retrieved the rags, and handed them out to all the people standing by the fence. A few campers looked at them, momentarily puzzled.

"Wave them!" Lisa yelled. "Anything to get the horses' attention and frighten them away from the barn instead of toward it!"

The campers followed her instructions. It seemed to help, but Lisa didn't think that it would be enough.

Then came two sounds that she had been expecting to hear—one bad, one good. The first was the collapse of the loft floor. There was a loud crash as it landed on the main floor of the barn, spreading the fire further and faster. The horses jumped back in surprise, but then quickly resumed their press toward the building.

The second sound was one of sirens. The Fire Department had arrived. The barn was burning too fast to be saved, especially since the loft had collapsed, but maybe the firemen could keep the fire from spreading.

Lisa returned to her work.

NEARBY, CAROLE WAS thinking as hard and as fast as she could. She'd never seen anything like the horses' frantic press to return to the barn, and she'd never seen horses less interested in nine people waving rags. If only just one horse would start to retreat, Carole was sure others would follow him to safety. Normally, waving a single rag would be enough to send a herd of horses on the run. She'd even witnessed Topside completely miss a jump in a horse show because a thoughtless spectator had waved her cloak.

Topside—where is Topside? Carole asked herself. Although Stevie was riding Topside at camp, Carole had ridden him at Pine Hollow a couple of times and she knew what a wonderfully obedient horse he was. Then it occurred to her that if she could get on Topside's back, she'd have a chance to convince him to run for safety—and maybe convince the rest of the herd as well.

Swiftly, she boosted herself up onto the fence. She just *had* to find Topside. Unfortunately, Topside was a bay horse, which meant he was brown with a black mane and tail—like almost every other horse in the paddock! Carole anxiously scanned the herd.

And there he was. Like the others, he was clearly

terrified. He was frightened by the sound and garish light of the fire, but he was also alarmed by what the other horses were doing.

"Here, boy," Carole said as calmly as she could. Horses, she knew, couldn't understand most words, but they were experts at tone of voice. She tried to keep her voice even and soothing. Topside's ears flicked toward her in response. She was just able to reach out and pat his neck. Then the throng of horses moved to one side, carrying Topside with them. His ears flattened again. Carole followed them, shifting her position on the fence.

She could do it, she was sure. She *had* to do it, but she sure needed help. The best help in the world with Topside was Stevie. *Where was she?*

THERE WERE EIGHT horses in the stable area of the barn's lower level. Stevie looked around. She was alone. She didn't have time to go for help. She was going to have to do this herself.

Common sense told her to release the horses farthest from the door first. She dashed in, ran for the most distant stall, opened the door, and tugged at the horse's halter. He whinnied a sound somewhere between angry and scared.

"I know just how you feel, boy," she said. Firmly, steadily, she led him to the door and walked him through it. As soon as she released his halter, she gave him a slap on the flank. He neighed loudly and took off in the direction of the pond. Stevie hoped the horses she released wouldn't run too far, but she hoped they'd run far enough. There would be plenty of time to find them, as long as they were alive.

Wasting no time, she went on to the next horse. In the eerie, orangish light, she thought she recognized him. Major! Lisa would be glad she'd saved him. Major followed the first horse off into the darkness.

In the split second before she returned to the barn, she heard the sound of the loft falling—and the Fire Department arriving. Maybe, maybe, she'd get some help from them. Maybe they'd be able to save some of the barn.

As Stevie rapidly led the horses out one by one, she thought about the camp's nice old barn—the cool feeling of the stable area on a hot summer day, the old-fashioned drive-through design, the tack room, and the other storage rooms with the wagons and the sled. She hoped some of those things would be saved. But horses came first.

Stevie kept looking for Teddy. She hadn't found him yet, but it was very hard to see in the stable area at all. She knew he was there. She wanted more than anything to get him out, but she couldn't waste time looking for just one horse. They all needed freedom.

And she needed time!

FOR ONCE, CAROLE was glad about Fred's carelessness. He'd left a lead rope slung over the fence instead of putting it away as he should have. It was just the thing Carole needed.

The next time the horses surged toward her, she slipped her hands between the slats of the fence and clipped the lead rope onto Topside's halter. It wasn't exactly a snaffle-bitted bridle, but it would have to do because it was all there was.

Then she reached one hand over the top of the fence, took the lead rope in that hand, and climbed up. She knew she wouldn't get a better opportunity than this.

Talking constantly, softly, surely, using his name, patting his neck, Carole slowly lowered herself onto Topside's back. She was in pajamas and barefoot. She had no saddle, no boots, no spurs, nothing to tell Topside she meant business, except her calves and her voice.

She gripped him with her legs to let him know she was on board and she was in charge now. She wanted him to feel that he didn't have to make any more decisions in this very frightening experience—Carole would do it for him.

"Okay, Topside," she said. She clucked her tongue.

His ears straightened right up. It was a good sign. It meant he heard her and was alert for other signals. "This is going to test your skills as a roundup horse and mine as a cowboy. We don't have any time to waste, so let's get down to business. Let's go."

She nudged his belly with her bare feet. He tensed under her. She felt his uncertainty. She didn't want him to be uncertain. She wanted him to follow her instructions without question. She kicked him. At that, Topside seemed ready to take orders from her, but by then Carole was in the middle of a sea of horses, with no place to go!

At that instant, the first gigantic arc of water reached upward from the other side of the barn, suddenly visible to the horses. As one, the animals stepped back in fear, opening up their ranks ever so slightly. Carole held her hands low and pulled on the lead rope and prayed that Topside would recognize the signal as if it were from a bridle with a bit. For a moment, he stood still. Then, slowly, carefully, he began to walk backwards.

"Good boy!" Carole said, and she meant it!

"OUCH!" STEVIE SAID. One skittish mare had just kicked her. She rubbed her shin. It was swelling already, but it wasn't bleeding. She'd be okay. The mare would be all right as well. Her skittishness was actually helping her, because it meant she was anxious to escape. As soon as Stevie unbolted the door to her stall, the mare hightailed it out of the barn to safety.

"Teddy, Teddy! Where are you?" she called, coughing. The smoke was beginning to billow down into the lower level. It was much harder to see than it had been just a few minutes before.

Stevie found a gray horse cowering in the corner of a stall. She reached in over the half-door, hooked her fingers through his halter, and pulled gently.

But there was nothing gentle about the horse's reaction. The horse reared on its hind legs, terrified, shrieking loudly. His movement was so sudden that he pulled Stevie right up off the ground and halfway over the edge of the door. She managed to release her fingers from the halter and backed out of the stall before the horse could land on her.

"Swell—I'm trying to give you a hand and you think this is the right time to get on your own two feet!"

It wasn't much of a joke, but it was the best Stevie could do. In fact, she was quite proud of the fact that she could still make a joke, even a feeble one, at a dreadful time like this.

"Listen, let's save the fun and games for tomorrow. Then you can do your Hi-ho-Silver imitation. I might even clap. For now, let's stick to routine. I tell you what to do, you do it."

The gray eyed her warily, but didn't protest when she snapped a lead on his halter. He also didn't move when she tugged at it. She tugged it harder. Then she yanked it. He yanked back. This horse wasn't going to budge.

One of the very first things a horse is taught to do, is to obey a halter lead rope. This horse was so upset and frightened that he had obviously forgotten everything he'd ever been taught. Stevie was trying to save his life, but he was acting as if she were trying to make him do something unpleasant, like lead him onto a van—

That was it! There were lots of tricks to putting horses on vans, and the first was a blindfold. Within a few seconds Stevie had torn off one of the legs of her pajamas. It was the only thing she had that would work, and besides, she'd never liked the little flowers on them. For a moment she imagined explaining to her mother what had happened to the pajamas. "See, we had this barn fire, Mom . . ." Stevie smiled to herself as she worked. Talking reassuringly to the gray horse, she slipped the homemade blindfold over his eyes. If he couldn't see anything, he'd have to rely on her. At least that was the idea.

It worked. Stevie tugged at the lead rope. One foot came forward. Before the horse knew what he was doing, he had followed Stevie out of the stall and was letting her lead him to the door. She took him all the way out of the barn before she took off his blindfold. She was afraid that once he could see, he might make his escape back into the barn. That would be awful.

"Get out of here!" Stevie yelled at the gray. She released the lead rope and slapped him hard on the rump. He looked over his shoulder at her with what she was sure was a dirty look. She whacked him again, harder. He bolted for freedom at full speed.

Now seven horses had been freed. *But where was Teddy?*

11

Once Carole was on Topside and Topside was paying attention to her, it began to seem as if everything were easy—especially when she had so much help from the other campers and the staff.

She got Topside to canter toward the herd, which made the horses shift over toward one side, even though they were still terrified of the fire. On Carole's signal, the campers at the fences began waving their towels. Eventually they got the horses' attention. Topside, whose bloodlines were one hundred percent Thoroughbred, now worked the horse herd like an experienced quarter horse. Quarter horses were the breed preferred by cowboys for their strength, stamina, speed, and intelligence. Topside was showing all these qualities. It was as if he understood the task before him, not just from command to command, but as a whole job. Topside began charging the herd and getting it to go in the right direction.

Not all the horses were cooperative. There were several who just wouldn't join the ranks as the herd began to back away from the barn.

Debbie saw the problem and found the solution. Her own horse, Bellevue, was one of those at the fence. Debbie found a way to climb up near him and, before he could object, she mounted him bareback. Holding his mane like reins, she began to ride him.

It was what Bellevue had needed, just like Topside. Debbie circled the herd, moving around to the side opposite Carole. When Carole approached the herd from one side, Debbie did the same from the other. Lisa and the other campers at the fence continued to wave.

Just three horses remained at the fence. One of them was Basil, whom Lisa had been riding just a few hours earlier. It seemed impossible that so much had happened in such a short period of time. Lisa glanced at the barn. This was no time to get philosophical. She hopped into the paddock and when she could get Basil's attention, she gave him a firm smack on his rear. It was just what he needed. Basil and the other three horses ran after the herd.

"Yahoo!" Nora called, running back to the fence. "You were fabulous."

"You did exactly the right thing!" Elsa said. The other campers standing by the fence applauded.

"It was teamwork," Lisa reminded them. "*We* were great. All of us."

"We're not done, though," Elsa said. "We brought everything we could find to make a fence, but now we've got to set it up. If we don't look out, we'll have every one of those horses back here in no time."

Lisa smiled to see that everybody who had been working with the herd was now joining Elsa in building a temporary fence. It had always been her experience that when people worked together, things got done. She was pretty sure this team could contain a mere herd of horses!

"Where are the horses?" someone asked. Lisa spun around. It was Phil.

"They're over on the other side of the hill," Lisa answered. "We got them away from the barn. They're safe now."

"All of them?" he asked.

"Sure, all of them," Lisa said. "You don't see any here now, do you?"

"Did you see Teddy? Was he there?" Phil asked.

"It's hard to tell them apart in the dark, Phil," Lisa said, with more patience than she felt. "But the horses that were in the paddock are safe. They're over the hill."

"But Teddy wasn't in the paddock," Phil said, almost stumbling over his words. "Stevie told me to put him in the barn—for the farrier."

Lisa had been concentrating so hard on the horses in the paddock that she'd completely forgotten about the horses in the barn. Phil's words reminded her that Major was in the barn, too. Major and Teddy were both in the barn—and where was Stevie?

"Oh, no!" Phil gasped. He ran. Lisa followed him. They couldn't get within thirty feet of the side entrance to the barn, though. The firemen wouldn't let them.

"Too dangerous," one said. "The whole side's about to go."

"But there's someone in there!" Phil said urgently.

"And it's my best friend!" Lisa added.

"Nobody's in there," the fireman said. "That would be crazy! Stand back now. And stay clear."

"TEDDY?"

The horse answered with a nicker. Stevie kept calling his name and followed the sound of his nicker to find him.

He was there all right, but Stevie knew as soon as

she found him that the fire might not be his worst problem.

Teddy was in a box stall, larger than the others. He was lying down, completely immobilized with terror. Experience had taught Stevie that every horse had his own distinct personality. At that moment, Teddy's wasn't helping him at all.

Stevie remembered how Phil had had trouble with Teddy when his foot hurt. She also remembered how she'd calmed him with her voice and gotten him to lift his foot. Now she had to do something similiar, only it was going to be very hard to sound reassuring with the fire crackling above her and the heat increasing every second. She didn't feel calm at all.

She started talking to the horse. She didn't think Teddy cared what she said, but he listened. She babbled on, not really aware of what she was saying, but as she spoke, she hooked on a lead rope and began matter-of-factly getting the frightened horse to his feet. She was surprised to find that she'd been telling him the story of Goldilocks and the Three Bears— Teddy Bears, of course.

At first, Teddy seemed to like it. Slowly but steadily, he rose to his feet. Then he stopped. He wouldn't move an inch. Stevie tried the makeshift blindfold. It didn't work. She tried tugging, then she tried yanking.

He wouldn't budge. Teddy felt secure in his box stall, and no matter how treacherous it really was, he didn't want to leave it.

But Teddy was also a trained riding horse, and there were some things which were always true about a riding horse. Stevie decided it might be the one way left that would work with Teddy. She entered the box stall, gave herself a boost on an overturned water bucket, and mounted Teddy. She was right about one thing. Once he had a rider on board, he wasn't going to stand still. Before Stevie even got a good grip on his mane, he was off!

The horse seemed to smell the fresh air and, having made up his mind that that was where he was going, wasted no time about it. He flew out of the barn, up the small incline of the entry path, and along the trail toward the pond. Stevie held on for dear life! This horse hadn't been named after the Rough Riders for nothing!

Most of the horses had headed for the pond. Stevie was certain Teddy would do the same. Teddy did, but he didn't stop at the beach the way the other seven horses from the barn had done. He kept on going at full gallop! The last voice Stevie heard as she and Teddy flew past the cabins was Phil's. It was faint but distinct.

"Stevie!"

Stevie was a good rider. She knew a lot about how to control a horse, how to make it do what she wanted, and how to keep it from doing what *it* wanted to do. But all of these things were difficult riding bareback without a bridle. On a still-terrified Teddy, they were impossible. There was only one thing she could do, and that was to hold on. The horse raced through the woods, snorting and sweating up a lather. He stumbled on rocks and roots, brushing up against branches, trees, and briars. Stevie's legs got scratched a dozen times and she could feel blood trickling down them. It didn't matter, though. The only thing that mattered was saving Teddy. As long as she was with him, there was a chance she could keep him from killing himself. Until he was ready to stop running, there wasn't much she could do, but she could be with him to calm him when he wore out. She clutched his thick mane with both hands, gripped his sleek belly with her cut legs, and leaned forward, making herself as small a target as possible for the branches that lashed at her body.

All the time she talked soothingly to the horse. "And then Goldilocks sat in the great big chair. 'Oh, no,' she said. 'This is much too big for me.'" She couldn't believe she was telling a fairy tale to a horse. It probably wasn't doing Teddy much good, but she knew she needed to talk. It was a way of keeping herself from being terrified, and it was a way of reminding him she was there—not that it was working very well for either of them.

Teddy was a big strong horse. Stevie was afraid he could keep on running for hours. She was more worried for his safety than for herself. Every time he stumbled on something, he risked seriously hurting himself. If the brambles and prickles were hurting her, she hated to think what they were doing to his beautiful and delicate legs. She'd once seen a horse hurt so badly that he'd been put down. She didn't want the same thing to happen to Teddy—especially not after she'd saved him from a fire!

Stevie clung tightly to his neck. She couldn't let Teddy get hurt. She just couldn't!

She kept on talking to him, and finally he began to slow down. His gallop wound down to a canter. It should have been an easy rocking gait, comfortable even bareback, but Teddy was lame. He stumbled with almost every step, now feeling the pain of wounds that had been numbed for a while by his terror.

The canter became a trot.

"Whoa there, boy," Stevie said. She tried shifting her weight, as she would have in a saddle, to signal him to stop. He slowed to a walk and then stopped.

Stevie made him walk until he cooled down and then she didn't move from his back until she was certain he wasn't going to take off again. They were in a clearing. She had no idea how far they were from camp or how they'd get back, but she could see that there was nothing for Teddy to fear in the clearing. The fire was a nightmare that was well out of sight, and, she hoped, out of mind.

She patted his neck soothingly, reassuringly. Teddy nodded his head in a familiar gesture. He was telling her that he was okay. She hoped he was right.

Slowly, Stevie slid down off his back. Moving carefully so as not to startle him, she checked him out. He had some nasty cuts on his legs, and the bruise on his hoof where she'd removed the stone was obviously bothering him a lot. Carrying her over all that rough terrain probably hadn't helped, either.

Stevie looked around and found that she and Teddy were right next to a stream. She tested the water. It was cool and seemed fresh. She led Teddy over to it and let him have a sip. Then she scooped up the cool water in her hands and began cleansing his wounds. He pulled back from her, so she began talking again.

"Once upon a time . . ."

Teddy stood still while Stevie finished washing his cuts, talking the whole time. She could see just well enough in the moonlight to be fairly certain the bleeding was slowing down in most of the cuts. One of the cuts, though, was more serious. Stevie looked around for something to use as a bandage. The obvious answer was her other pajama leg—after all, she'd already sacrificed the first as a blindfold.

It did the trick. She wrapped it carefully around Teddy's leg and tied it securely. Within a few minutes, the bleeding stopped.

"Don't get into any more trouble, okay?" Stevie told Teddy. "Unlike you, I've only got two legs. I'm completely out of spare pajama parts!" She sighed. As long as she could joke, she was fine.

Stevie knew she ought to try to go back to camp. She knew people would be worried about her and Teddy, but she also knew she and Teddy were tired, very tired. The last thing they needed now was to wander through the woods and get even more lost than they already were. She secured Teddy's lead rope on a branch near some wild grass that he could snack on, and sat down, leaning against a pine tree. She'd rest for just a minute.

The next thing Stevie knew, it was broad daylight. She was startled awake by the sound of her own name.

"Stevie! You're all right!" Phil said, kneeling beside her.

She smiled weakly. "Yes, I am, and so is Teddy, though he's got some cuts. I tried to bandage one of them—" she tried to explain. She wanted to assure Phil that everything was okay, but he didn't give her a chance.

"Shut up," he said, nearly whispering. "Because I can't apologize to you if you're doing all the talking."

Stevie didn't say a word.

"You're good at taking care of horses. You're also good at riding them. You're a true friend, Stevie Lake, and I'll be honored to be in the same horse show with you when the time comes and I won't be surprised if you win every ribbon there is because you've got more guts than anybody I've ever known. What I'm trying to say is I think you're terrific. I think you're the greatest girl I ever met, and I don't want you to be mad at me anymore."

"I don't care about the horse show," Stevie said wearily. "All I care about is the horses. And I'm not mad at you," she promised. "Boy, I'm tired. I hope I'm not dreaming you're here. How did you find us anyway?"

"We knew about what direction you'd taken off in, so Barry and I drove this way. You weren't hard to spot. You're only about ten feet from the road. We brought a van, so we can take you and Teddy back to camp right now."

Stevie stood up and looked around, seeing the locale for the first time. If she'd known about the road in the dark, she might have been tempted to try to return on her own. She was glad she hadn't. She couldn't have walked another step. Neither could Teddy.

"Now about my horse," Phil said. "I hope he hasn't gotten too used to flowered bandages. Do you think the other horses will make fun of him?"

Stevie smiled. It felt very good to know that Phil could still joke, too.

12

STEVIE REALLY WANTED to see Lisa and Carole. There was so much to say, so much to tell them.

As Barry drove the van into camp, Stevie got her first look at the burned barn. Like many fires, it had done some unpredictable damage. The loft was completely gone and a lot of the main floor had been destroyed. Some parts had hardly been touched, though. The tack room, for instance, was dusty, smoky, and soaked from the firemen's hoses, but the tack would be fine after a good cleaning.

"Oh, that's great!" Stevie said. "That means we can still have our classes today!"

Barry looked at her sternly. "I think that today any rider who spent the night saving the lives of eight horses and tending to another in the pitch-black forest, ripping up her pajamas—to say nothing of her legs—just to protect a horse's, should definitely take the day off. Besides, there's something else you should see."

Phil had brought along a pair of Stevie's sneakers. She was glad to have them as she walked around the charred beams that lay scattered on the ground. She was even more glad to have them when Phil took her hand and led her to the barn's lower entrance.

It was the same place she'd been just a few hours earlier. She remembered what had happened so clearly that she could almost feel the presence of the terrified horses and her own fear. She could hear their anxious cries, the nervous stomping of their feet in the dim light of the lower stable. It was the same place, but it didn't look like it at all. It had been transformed into a yawning, pitch-black hole. Nothing was left of it except a few metal pieces that had survived the fire. Stevie picked up a charred bucket handle.

"Right after you and Teddy made your exit, the main floor collapsed in this section. The whole area was totally destroyed, and if you hadn't been here to save the horses, they would have been destroyed as well," Barry told her.

"And if you hadn't done such a fast job of it—" Phil began.

"I get the picture," Stevie interrupted. She didn't

want him to say the words. She began shivering, and the full weight of the work she'd done and the danger she'd barely escaped came crashing down on her. "Um, maybe I should go lie down," she said a little unsteadily.

"Here, I'll help you." And Phil leaned over and picked her up, just like that!

Stevie sighed contentedly. This was definitely the most romantic thing that had ever happened to her. She rested her head on Phil's shoulder and was nearly asleep by the time she reached Cabin Three.

THE SADDLE CLUB Meeting that afternoon lasted a long time. This Saddle Club Meeting was very different, though, because every single camper at Moose Hill was included. They each brought a pile of tack, a tin of saddle soap, water, and extra sponges. They found a shady spot near the mess hall and began to work, talking as they cleaned tack.

Stevie told everybody all about her adventures in the lower barn.

"You were a hero!" Lisa declared.

Stevie shook her head. "No way. I wasn't waving towels at a frightened herd of horses who could have trampled you in a second. And I didn't mount one of those horses in the paddock. Now *that* was heroic."

"You should have seen the fence builders, Stevie,"

Carole put in. "While some of us herded the horses, the rest put up a fence, instantly. They could have been trampled, too."

Stevie smiled a little to herself.

"What's so funny, Stevie?" Nora asked her.

Stevie shrugged. "Carole and Lisa and I decided long ago that what makes us friends is that we're all horse crazy. I think it may be true of all of us—this whole group. Being horse crazy made us do the things we did last night, and look at us now." There were smiles and nods of agreement. "On the other hand," Stevie continued, "if you *really* think about what we did last night, you'd have to conclude that we're all actually just *plain* crazy!" Everybody laughed. It was a wonderful sound.

Barry joined the group then. He sat down, picked up a bridle, and began soaping it.

"There are a couple of things you should know," he informed the campers. "The firemen pinpointed the start of the fire, and there's no doubt about it—it began in the moldy hay in the loft. What happens with moldy hay is that the process of rotting creates heat and oxygen. I don't want to get too technical, but at some point, there's enough heat and enough oxygen so that the whole thing begins to smolder. It doesn't take much to start hay burning. Every stable manager knows it. And now you've seen the consequences. I'd given instructions to have the moldy hay removed from the loft, but apparently those instructions weren't followed. The person responsible for that has left camp."

Lisa had figured as much when she'd seen Fred earlier that day, angrily dumping his duffel bags into a station wagon and leaving camp.

"There is a bright side to all of this, though. First, and most important, all the horses are safe. There are minor injuries to take care of, but thanks to quick thinking and action on everyone's part, the horses are okay.

"The other bright side is that although I loved that old barn, with its wonderful hayloft and smooth wooden floors, it was a barn, not a stable. I'll be able to rebuild with the insurance money and we'll have a real stable. It'll be better than ever when you all return next year.

"Now, the final thing I want to say is that some of you have been concerned about the horse show and the judges who will be working with me and—"

Debbie interrupted him. "Barry, can I say something before you continue?"

For a second, Barry looked dubious. "Sure," he said.

"I was acting dumb and selfish and I apologize for questioning the judging. Don't make any changes, okay?"

Barry paused before speaking. "I wasn't going to," he said. "But I'm glad you agree."

Lisa smiled. Debbie had come a long way from the girl who had had an argument with Barry just the day before. Actually, everybody had. It hadn't taken much, Lisa thought to herself. Just a barn fire, terrified horses, courage, bravery, and the total cooperation of about thirty people who had previously viewed everyone else as a competitor instead of a teammate. No trouble at all.

13

LISA WASN'T CERTAIN whether it was more fun to get ready for a horse show or to be in one. All she knew was that she was having a great time.

"You look like an old pro," Carole said, admiring Lisa's outfit.

"I'm not, but my clothes *are*," she joked. "I had to borrow gloves from Elsa, and I'm carrying a riding crop that Jack needs right after me. It belongs to Phil."

That was the way the show was going. Everybody was pitching in to see that all the riders did the best they could. And all of them *were* doing their best.

"Well, good luck on the jumps," Carole said.

"Thanks," Lisa said. She might need some. After all, she'd only been jumping since camp started. But she didn't really care if she took a ribbon. There were other beginners who were better than she was. She was just glad for the chance to show what she'd learned in ten days.

"Smile," Betty said to her, breaking her train of thought. "You're on!"

As soon as Barry called her name, she nudged Major into the ring. She circled it once, paused to tip her hat to the judges, just as she was supposed to, and then began her exercise.

Major loved it, but Lisa loved it even more. She had four jumps to go over. None of them was high, but her style and form were more important than how high she jumped. Major cantered gracefully toward the first jump. Just as she'd practiced a hundred times before, she rose in the saddle, leaned forward, held her hands by Major's neck, and gave him as much rein as she thought he would need. At precisely the right moment, Major rose in the air and, it seemed to Lisa, flew right over the poles. He landed softly, and she shifted her weight and slid back into the saddle. *Perfect!*

After that, nothing else mattered to Lisa. If she'd fallen off at the next jump she wouldn't have cared. She'd done one jump exactly right and she was proud of herself. Other people seemed to agree. Carole and Stevie and the rest of the campers were clapping for her. They all knew how much work that one jump represented. All that practice, all those hours had been worth it. As it turned out, she didn't have to worry about the other three jumps. They went just fine. Lisa had the feeling, though, that no jump she ever made would feel quite as good as the first perfect one she made in a show.

STEVIE SMOOTHED HER jacket while she and Topside waited their turn.

"Stephanie Lake!" Barry announced. Time to go.

Stevie and Topside had already competed in the Intermediate Jumping and Conformation events. Now, they were in Dressage. This event tested the training of both the horse and the rider. It was an opportunity for both Topside and Stevie to show good balance, concentration, and obedience. It was sometimes hard for casual viewers to see what was happening, especially when it was done well, because in Dressage, the horse had to respond to nearly invisible commands from the rider.

Stevie entered the ring, saluted the judges, and started her prepared ride. Her routine had been designed to show Topside off to best advantage, and as she began, her head was swimming with dozens of terms she'd been studying, like rhythm, cadence, hocks engaged, collection, and, most of all, impulsion. Topside didn't know any of those words, but he did everything perfectly. Together they made circles and curves at walk, trot, and canter. Stevie changed diagonals and leads, and their transitions were smooth as glass. Topside was in top form. Stevie couldn't help grinning triumphantly. By the time she finished her stationary turns, one pivoting on a foreleg, another on a hindleg, Stevie knew she'd been perfect.

She completed her exercise and rode out of the ring to the sound of applause. She didn't waste any time gloating about it, though. There was a lot of work to do. Since Teddy's legs were still healing, Phil was riding Topside, too. They had to adjust the leathers for his lanky frame.

"He's great," Stevie said to Phil, patting Topside lovingly. "You'll be fine. You're better at this stuff than I am, and Topside's better than both of us."

"I don't care about that now, Stevie," Phil said. "Really."

"Me, too," she said, and she meant it. "It was really dumb, that idea we had about taking all the ribbons. It wasn't any better than what Elsa and Debbie were doing. We should have known better. Riding is for having a good time."

"You got that right," he agreed. "By the way, I heard that Elsa and Debbie asked Barry if we could all go out on another camp-out tonight after the show, and he said yes. Still got those marshmallows?"

"Philip Marston!" Barry announced.

"You're up!" Stevie said, nodding in answer to his question. "Go get 'em!"

CAROLE WAS IN all the advanced classes with both Elsa and Debbie. Only two other riders were in those classes, because the advanced riders were so experienced.

Lisa, Stevie, and Phil watched them in awe.

"This is so great!" Lisa said. "I mean, having this chance to see kids who are so good. That big horse show we went to in New York was fantastic, but in a way I think this is even better. Those people at the show were almost professional riders, way better than I'll ever be. But these guys are really good riders and they're my age. It's fabulous."

"You mean *she's* fabulous," Stevie said, watching Debbie go over the jumps. "See how her body sort of folds when she gets ready to jump? It isn't exactly leaning forward. It's just about perfect."

"Wow," Lisa said, admiring Debbie's skill. "She's as good as she said she was."

"You're only ever as good as you are," Stevie pointed out. "Talking doesn't make you better. She learned that."

"We *all* did," Phil said.

Then it was Carole's turn. She was wonderful, too.

Lisa had watched her jump a lot, but she'd never seen her do better. When Carole was finished, there was a lot of applause. And nobody clapped louder than the other riders in the event.

At most shows, Lisa knew, ribbons were awarded immediately after each event. Barry had decided to do it differently. She suspected he wanted to minimize their importance, but he needn't have worried. At the end of the show, many riders almost forgot to come to the awards ceremony. It just wasn't important. What was important to each and every one of them was that they'd all learned and had a chance to show what they'd learned.

There were plenty of ribbons to go around. Lisa, Stevie, and Carole had each done well in their events and had blue and red ribbons to take with them. They were pleased, but they were also pleased when their friends got ribbons as well. They knew their accomplishments couldn't be measured in just ribbons.

One thing that could be measured, though, was how much they all wanted to cool off in the pond before their final night at camp.

"Last one in has to pick up all the kindling tonight!" Jack shouted. It didn't take any of them long to get into the water.

CAROLE TOLD ANOTHER ghost story at the camp

fire. This one was about Frankenstallion. The campers
made s'mores as they listened, joining in with sugges-
tions as the story progressed. They all laughed as Frankenstallion ended up marrying Marezilla and they had
a baby named Dracufoal.

After a while, the campers began singing songs, starting, naturally, with the theme song from the Munsters.
Stevie sat next to Lisa and Carole. Phil was nearby.

He tapped Stevie's shoulder. "Want to go for a
walk?" he asked. Quietly, they sneaked away from the
camp fire. They didn't do such a good job of sneaking,
though, because as soon as they were standing, all the
other campers turned and began waving good-bye to
them.

Stevie blushed. "I've had enough of fires," she began
to explain. "See, I had this frightening experience—"

"Let's just go, Stevie," Phil said. He smiled and took
her hand and they left, hearing the teasing laughter
behind them.

"I can't believe it's almost over," Stevie said. "Two
weeks seemed like such a long time, but now, *poof!* It's
done. But so much has happened in two weeks. All
those classes, the first camp-out, the fire, the show,
and now our last camp-out."

"Last camp-out? No way," Phil said. "I think we'll
be back next summer for more of them, and I think
we'll be seeing each other in between."

Stevie certainly hoped so.

She and Phil walked to the edge of the temporary paddock where the horses were housed for the night. A stream flowed along one side of it. They sat at the edge of the stream, took off their shoes, and dangled their feet in the cool water.

Stevie and Phil were silent for a long time. The field ran uphill and several of the horses stood on the top of the hill, silhouetted against the cool, deep blue sky by the moon beyond them. One rose his head and nickered. Another responded, nuzzling at his shoulder. Stevie could hear the horses nearby munch on fresh hay and grass contentedly. There were other night sounds—the brook, crickets, even an owl.

Stevie thought that this was maybe the most beautiful place in the world. She looked at Phil. There was just one more thing that could make it more beautiful. And at that moment, he leaned toward her and kissed her for the first time.

14

"HE KISSED YOU!" Lisa almost shrieked. The girls were back in Willow Creek, gathered at the edge of Stevie's swimming pool, sharing secrets. Camp was over, but they had all acquired enough memories to last a lifetime!

Stevie nodded excitedly. Telling her friends about her first kiss was *almost* as much fun as doing it.

"Like, on the lips?" Carole said.

Stevie nodded. "You're not jealous, are you?" she asked a little anxiously, suddenly aware that she was the first of them to be kissed by a boy.

"Jealous?" Lisa repeated. "Of course I'm jealous, but one of us had to be first and Phil's a really neat guy, so I'm glad it was you."

"Me, too," Stevie grinned.

"I don't mind, either," Carole reassured her. "But tell me about it again—you know, the part about the horses on the hill?"

Stevie laughed. For now anyway, horses were still more important to Carole than boys, but Carole was glad her friend was happy, and that was fine with Stevie. Stevie told her again about the horses on the hill.

"It must have been beautiful," Carole sighed.

"It was," Stevie said. "Believe me, it was."

"Uh-oh, here she goes looking all lovesick again," Lisa teased her. "Remember, Stevie, how Carole had to bail you out of making a fool of yourself in class by getting you to have a coughing fit?"

"I remember, I remember," Stevie said. "And I promise I'll never do it again. Well, maybe never."

Carole and Lisa laughed. It was nice having Stevie back to normal again.

Lisa wanted to make sure Stevie didn't leave anything out, so she pumped her some more about her walk with Phil. Carole was a little distracted; she'd been thinking about something else.

"Tired of the four hundredth go-round of Stevie's first kiss?" Lisa asked, noticing that Carole's attention had slipped.

"Oh, no," Carole grinned. "I'm ready for four-oh-one any time, but I was remembering something else, too. Remember how Kate Devine told us she'd quit competitive riding because the competitiveness was keeping her from having any fun? I think we had more than a taste of that our first week at camp, and she's right. That's no way to ride!"

Lisa began combing her hair. "No, the best part about riding is doing what The Saddle Club does. We help one another."

"Right," Stevie said. "Just the way all of the campers were doing by the time of the show. It was great. It was like having twenty-seven more members of The Saddle Club."

Carole looked surprised. "Would you really want twenty-seven more members?" she asked.

"No way!" Lisa said. "I like us just the way we are. At least that's my vote."

"Maybe not *twenty-seven* more members," Stevie said thoughtfully. "But how about one more?"

Lisa and Carole didn't have to ask her who she meant. Friends just knew those things.

ABOUT THE AUTHOR

BONNIE BRYANT is the author of more than thirty books for young readers, including the best-selling novelizations of *The Karate Kid* movies. The Saddle Club books are her first for Bantam Skylark. She wrote her first book seven years ago and has been busy at her word processor ever since. (For her first three years as an author, Ms. Bryant was also working in the office of a publishing company. In 1986, she left her job to write full-time.)

Whenever she can, Ms. Bryant goes horseback riding in her hometown, New York City. She's had many riding experiences in the city's Central Park that have found their way into her Saddle Club books—and lots which haven't!

The author has two sons, and they all live together in an apartment in Greenwich Village that is just too small for a horse.

Saddle up for great reading with

THE SADDLE CLUB

A blue-ribbon series by Bonnie Bryant

Stevie, Carole and Lisa are all very different, but they *love* horses! The three girls are best friends at Pine Hollow Stables, where they ride and care for all kinds of horses. Come to Pine Hollow and get ready for all the fun and adventure that comes with being 13!

Don't miss this terrific 10-book series. Collect them all!

- ☐ 15594 HORSE CRAZY #1 ....$2.75
- ☐ 15611 HORSE SHY #2....................................$2.75
- ☐ 15626 HORSE SENSE #3................................$2.75
- ☐ 15637 HORSE POWER #4 ....$2.75
- ☐ 15703 TRAIL MATES #5................................$2.75
- ☐ 15728 DUDE RANCH #6................................$2.75
- ☐ 15754 HORSE PLAY #7 ....$2.75
- ☐ 15769 HORSE SHOW #8 ....$2.75
- ☐ 15780 HOOF BEAT #9....................................$2.75
- ☐ 15790 RIDING CAMP #10 ....$2.75

Watch for other SADDLE CLUB books all year. More great reading—and riding to come!

Buy them at your local bookstore or use this handy page for ordering.

From Bantam-Skylark Books
IT'S

From Betsy Haynes, the bestselling author of the Taffy Sinclair books, *The Great Mom Swap*, and *The Great Boyfriend Trap*, comes THE FABULOUS FIVE. Follow the adventures of Jana Morgan and the rest of THE FABULOUS FIVE as they begin the new school year in Wakeman Jr. High.

☐	SEVENTH-GRADE RUMORS (Book #1)	15625-X	$2.75
☐	THE TROUBLE WITH FLIRTING (Book #2)	15633-0	$2.75
☐	THE POPULARITY TRAP (Book #3)	15634-9	$2.75
☐	HER HONOR, KATIE SHANNON (Book #4)	15640-3	$2.75
☐	THE BRAGGING WAR (Book #5)	15651-9	$2.75
☐	THE PARENT GAME (Book #6)	15670-5	$2.75
☐	THE KISSING DISASTER (Book #7)	15710-8	$2.75
☐	THE RUNAWAY CRISIS (Book #8)	15719-1	$2.75
☐	THE BOYFRIEND DILEMMA (Book #9)	15720-5	$2.75
☐	PLAYING THE PART (Book #10)	15745-0	$2.75
☐	HIT AND RUN (Book #11)	15746-9	$2.75
☐	KATIE'S DATING TIPS (Book #12)	15748-5	$2.75
☐	THE CHRISTMAS COUNTDOWN (Book #13)	15756-6	$2.75
☐	SEVENTH-GRADE MENACE (Book #14)	15763-9	$2.75
☐	MELANIE'S IDENTITY CRISIS (Book #15)	15775-2	$2.75
☐	THE HOT-LINE EMERGENCY (Book #16)	15781-7	$2.75
☐	CELEBRITY AUCTION (Book #17)	15784-1	$2.75

Buy them at your local bookstore or use this page to order:

Bantam Books, Dept. SK28, 414 East Golf Road, Des Plaines, IL 60016

Please send me the items I have checked above. I am enclosing $_____ (please add $2.00 to cover postage and handling). Send check or money order, no cash or C.O.D.s please.

Mr/Ms _____

Address _____

City/State _____ Zip _____

SK28-4/90

Please allow four to six weeks for delivery.
Prices and availability subject to change without notice.

Great FREE offer
just for you!

Join SNEAK PEEKS™!

Do you want to know what's new before anyone else? Do you like to read great books about girls just like you? If you do, then you won't want to miss SNEAK PEEKS™! Be the first of your friends to know what's hot ... When you join SNEAK PEEKS™, we'll send you FREE inside information in the mail about the latest books ... *before they're published!* Plus updates on your favorite series, authors, and exciting new stories filled with friendship and fun ... adventure and mystery ... girlfriends and boyfriends.

It's easy to be a member of SNEAK PEEKS™. Just fill out the coupon below ... and get ready for fun! It's FREE! Don't delay—sign up today!

Mail to: SNEAK PEEKS™
       Bantam Books, P.O. Box 1011,
       South Holland, IL 60473

☐ YES! I want to be a member of Bantam's SNEAK PEEKS™ and receive hot-off-the-press information in the mail.

Name _____ Birthdate _____

Address _____

City/State _____ Zip _____

SK31-10/89

PLAYING TO WIN!

"Because of unforeseen scheduling problems, the match is going to take place on Saturday," said Max.

"This *week?*" Stevie screeched. "But we won't be ready. We'll never win!"

"No, I'm sure we won't," Max said quite calmly. "I wouldn't expect us to win our first match in any event. So think of it as an intense practice rather than a real match."

This was more than Stevie could handle. As soon as the practice chukka started, Stevie started too—on the players.

Lisa and Carole waited on the sidelines to be called in to play. "It was bad enough when she thought the match against Phil's club was going to be in two weeks. Now that it's this week, there's no stopping her," Lisa complained.

"When Stevie gets an idea in her head—"

"I know, I know. Even an atom bomb can't blast it out. But if she doesn't stop being so awful to everybody, somebody's going to go to a lot of trouble to find an atom bomb somewhere—"

"If we don't just strangle her with our bare hands first," Carole finished the sentence for Lisa.

Other Bantam Skylark Books you will enjoy
Ask your bookseller for the books you have missed

ANASTASIA KRUPNIK by Lois Lowry

ANNE OF GREEN GABLES by L. M. Montgomery

BIG RED by Jim Kjelgaard

THE DOUBLE FUDGE DARE by Louise Ladd

THE GHOST IN THE ATTIC (Haunting with Louisa #1)
by Emily Cates

THE GHOST WORE GRAY by Bruce Coville

GOING HOME by Nicholasa Mohr

THE GREAT TV TURNOFF (The Fabulous Five #24)
by Betsy Haynes

THE ORPHAN GAME by Barbara Cohen

PICK OF THE LITTER by Mary Jane Auch

THE SARA SUMMER by Mary Downing Hahn

SEAL CHILD by Sylvia Peck

THE WILD MUSTANG by Joanna Campbell

THE WORLDWIDE DESSERT CONTEST by Dan Elish